A QUARTERLY SCIENCE FICTION & FANTASY MAGAZINE

ISSUE # 14 SPRING 2020

CONTENTS

Shaun Kilgore, Editor and Publisher

Published by Founders House Publishing LLC
614 Wayne Street, Suite 200A
Danville, IL 61832

www.mythicmag.com
www.foundershousepublishing.com

MYTHIC is quarterly magazine. We publish speculative fiction, specifically science fiction and fantasy. Our mission is to expand the range of what is currently possible within both genres. We like new perspectives and new spins on familiar tropes. Diversity is a hallmark of our vision.

ISBN 13: 978-1-945810-49-7

Printed in the United States of America

A Special Thanks

I want to include a shout out to our **Patreon Patrons**!

Elena Westbrook, Isabel Kunkle, Jay Skiles, Mariah Jensen, Richard Ohnemus, Dave Ring, David England, Robert Walshe, Matt McNeill, Grant Martin, Jonathan Hodge, Mary Jane Kilgore, Scott Noel, Jeff Harrison, Mark Akins, Jonathan Eaton, Matt Hopper, James Rumpel, Randell Pinegar, Robert Mathesien, Tom Jolly, Justin Patrick Moore, Daniel S, Edward Matalka, Erik Jay Weber, and Ian Chung.

Your contributions are helping me to offer a whole new selection of imaginative and engaging science fiction and fantasy stories in every issue of MYTHIC. I also want to thank those who've subscribed to MYTHIC and supported us in other ways.

Help us pay our authors better rates for their stories and make MYTHIC a better magazine. Join us. Consider supporting MYTHIC on a monthly basis by becoming a Patron through Patreon and receive exclusive offers and other rewards.

For more information you can visit our Patreon page at: **www.patreon.com/mythicmag**

LOVE IN THE RUINS

TALES OF ROMANCE IN THE DEINDUSTRIAL FUTURE

EDITED BY

JOHN MICHAEL GREER

"In times of such huge confusion, the little things go on. During the 'Ten Days that Shook the World' the cafés and theaters of Moscow and Petrograd stayed open, people fell in love, sued each other, died, shed sweat and tears; and some of the tears were tears of laughter."
~ Theodore Sturgeon, "The Hurkle is a Happy Beast"

Many stories have been written already about the approaching end of industrial civilization: about the great tragedies and the small triumphs, about struggles spread out across landscapes and struggles just as bitter within individual hearts, about the people who survive and the ones who don't. One theme that's been unfairly neglected in deindustrial fiction is love. As iconic SF author Theodore Sturgeon noted, the little things go on—and among those little things are human relationships, blossoming in the most unlikely settings. This anthology includes ten stories and three poems about love in the deindustrial future, by turns ethereal and earthy, traumatic and tender—but all of them ending with a promise of happily ever after...

Editor's Note

By Shaun Kilgore

A new issue has arrived. It's the the fourteen issue of the quarterly magazine I started back in 2016—and the second to last one I will be doing in that format.

This year has been challenging. Yes, I know that an understatement given the state of things in the world. A global pandemic, an economic crisis and a tumultuous election year here in the U.S. have heaped all sort of difficulties on just about everyone. It's been no exception for me.

For the last few months, I've been struggling as an indie publisher just trying to make ends meet and one of the difficulties of running a business is evaluating the various projects that take up my time and assessing whether they are worth continuing. I had to do that with MYTHIC. Admittedly this always been more of a passion project than a fully financially viable one.

As MYTHIC was operating, I had to consider the real possibilty that I would have to shutter it and move on from it. I almost did. But a few supporters chimed in and made me pause. I considered that there might be a different way to continue the magazine—provided that I had a bit more help.

So, this issue, number 14, is the second to last one that will be published as a quarterly magazine in print and eBook formats. Issue 15, the last quarterly, will follow and then I will be changing MYTHIC over to a bi-monthly publication that will include online content as well as the print and eBook editions. Does this mean that MYTHIC is out of the woods or safe from cancellation? No it doesn't.

As I write, I am planning a Kickstarter campaign for the new format that will serve a subscription drive. Gaining new fans and subscribers key for me to continuing serving up great sci-fi and fantasy fiction on a regular basis. Another aspect is maintaining and growing the patrons supporting MYTHIC via Patreon.com.

This is what it comes down to: I'm not ready to close the book on MYTHIC. Please join me on this journey. Thanks.

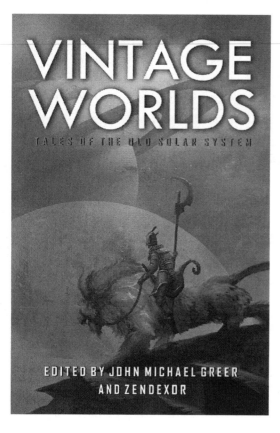

No One Returns From Tobed Aun

By John Michael Greer

They pulled the rough black cloth off Dammal's eyes, untied his hands, and took away the yellow garment of shame they'd put on him in Atal Thrau, leaving him naked. He blinked, tried to focus. Dark shapes around him turned into four men and two women in black Knowers' robes, all of them armed with iron-shod staves. Beyond them the lush foliage of the jungle spread over tumbled stones, clambered up walls the centuries had not yet leveled. Gaudily colored birds fluttered and darted across a blue sky far above.

"This is far enough," said the Eldest, a hollow-cheeked old man with hard unforgiving eyes. "Talith, you know what to do."

"Yes, Eldest," said one of the women.

The Eldest motioned with his head and walked away. Four others followed him. Dammal watched them go until the trail they followed took them out of sight behind a heap of half-overgrown stones.

"A waste of time," said the woman then.

Dammal turned and considered her. Tall and rawboned, she held her staff with an easy familiarity that warned him she knew how to use it. Talith, she thought, Talith daughter of Eleli. He'd watched her now and then since he went through the rites of manhood; she was smart and tough, nothing like the soft stupid chattering women his family kept trying to talk him into marrying. Their families had exchanged bridegrooms more than once in past generations, too. If she'd been closer to his age, he might well have scandalized everyone in Atal Thrau by talking to his grandmothers about talking to her grandmothers, but she was six years older than he was and the rules the Knowers taught demanded that he marry within his age-set or not at all.

He stifled a bitter laugh, knowing that none of that mattered now.

"I'm supposed to lecture you about your crime," she said then. "Another waste of time. You know what you did as well as anyone, and you also know what's going to happen next. If you try to go back the way the others went, they'll be waiting."

Dammal found his voice. "If I go any other way the Gath'talla will be waiting."

She gave him the same tired look the loremasters gave a pupil who gave

7

the same wrong answer too many times. "You should have thought of that a long time ago."

That was true enough, he knew. He said nothing.

"My task is to wait and watch here," she said then, "so your family will know." She considered him for a moment. "It's proper to give you some advice. Stay away from metal unless you want to die right away. Metal calls it. If you stay away from that and you're lucky—very, very lucky—you might just reach the Sanctuary, and then you're no concern of ours."

"And if I defeat the Gath'talla and return?"

That got him the tired look again. "No one returns from Tobed Aun."

He tried to think of something to say to that, but no words came. After a moment, he made the gesture-of-parting, turned, and started down the half-overgrown trail before him.

Birds fluttered overhead and the jungle drowsed under the weight of midday as Dammal, a lithe brown shadow among deeper shadows, made his way into the vast crumbling pile of Tobed Aun. He'd found a long straight branch of dabh-wood, used a broken cobble to cut it from the tree and sharpen one end to a point that could readily pierce flesh. Whether it would serve against the thing that waited in the ruins he did not know, but feeling the heft of it in his hand made him a little less uneasy as he moved deeper into the city.

For it had been a city once, or so he'd been taught by the loremasters. People had lived there back in the gray morning of time, when all things were different, when the wise and wicked Knowers of that far-off age called thunder-spirits down out of the sky and bound them to strange service. Then the wise and wicked ones perished, terrible things descended from the skies to dwell in the empty houses, and for countless seasons Tobed Aun lay desolate, the haunt of wild beasts and birds, and of something else. No one went there willingly, and those who went otherwise—

Talith's final words whispered in his mind, mocking. He shook his head angrily, ducked under a low branch, kept going.

From the wooden palisade that surrounded Atal Thrau, the ruined city was a dim uneven shape on the horizon, veiled by mist more often than not. Still, Dammal searched his memories, recalled ragged spires visible at sunset, black against the red sky. The Sanctuary at the heart of Tobed Aun was a place of spires that strove toward the heavens, all the old stories said that, and said also that the last of the Ancients still dwelt there. If he got there before the Gath'talla found him, he might be safe in their company. Now to find where the Sanctuary was...

A mass of stone overgrown with vines emerging out of the tangled jungle ahead, the last remnant of some ancient building, offered a view above the trees. Dammal paused at the foot, then walked halfway around it, made sure that it harbored no obvious danger, and leaned his makeshift spear against the stone. A bound upward in a likely place and a few moments of scrambling got him up the ragged outward face to a cornice well above the trail. From there he clambered higher, sending birds squawking and fluttering away, until finally he stood atop the summit and raised a hand to shield his eyes from the rays of the midday sun.

There the spires were, great ragged shapes rising above the jungle in the distance. Haze veiled them but could not conceal fallen walls, windows empty as the eyes of skulls. Staring at them, Dammal felt a glimmer of hope. If all went well, he might reach them by nightfall.

The wind shifted suddenly, and brought a troubling scent: the lightning-smell, sharp and unmistakable. A glance showed no cloud in the sky, though, so it could not be lightning.

The Gath'talla, then.

He clambered back down to the edge, dropped to the trail, picked up his spear again and started toward the distant spires.

T he sun was still high above him when he found the first corpse, or what was left of it.

He'd found a street, or something like one, running straight as a thrown spear between tumbled masses of stone. It was wide enough that the trees didn't quite meet over it, and the spires that he hoped might mark the Sanctuary hovered in the gap, pale with mist and distance. He set himself a steady pace, swift enough to give him some hope of reaching the spires before sunset, slow enough that he could attend to every jungle noise and stray scent that reached him.

Only once did he break his pace, and that was when he passed an upright stone that broke free of the clinging vines, and saw writing on it. His first impulse was to stop and try to puzzle out what message the ornate characters spelled out; his second was to hurry on past, head down, and hope no one had seen him. He caught himself and laughed aloud, thinking: even if they are here, and they are not, what does it matter if they find me at it again? How can they bring me here when I am here already?

Still, he dared not spend the time to try to read it, and the strips of barkcloth on which he'd daubed the characters he knew, along with little pictures of what they meant, had gone into the flames the Knowers kindled once they caught him. Only those who wore the black robe were permitted to learn letters, that was another of the Knowers' rules, and those who broke any of their rules risked the fate they had sent Dammal to face.

You know what you did, Talith had said. A smoldering anger kindled in him as he recalled the words, and he flung a thought back toward her: do you know why? Do you know that I wanted to become a Knower and they refused me, because my parents are poor, because I ask questions others don't?

No one answered, and the delay brought the spires no closer. Dammal turned sharply away from the stone, started along the street again. He had just settled back into his pace when sun on a blackened patch ahead of him caught his attention. He kept moving, but a moment later saw what it was, and slowed.

There in the middle of the street lay the sprawled fragments of a human skeleton. The small and fragile bones had long since surrendered to the savage heat and damp of the jungle, but the skull and a few other larger bones remained. They were blackened as though burnt, and the stone on which they lay had been scorched as well. Dammal stared, then made the gesture-of-blessing to turn away the evil and hurried on.

That grim reminder soon vanished into haze and shadow behind him, and the dread he felt had just begun to lessen when he passed another. A third appeared when the second was still just in sight, and thereafter he came upon them more often. Most of the skeletons were little more than fragments, but now and then he passed one that had seen much less exposure; here and there, too, he caught faint burned marks on the paving of the street with no skeleton atop them, and guessed that someone's bones had lain there at some more distant time. That troubled him; everyone knew the Knowers sent those who defied their rules to Tobed Aun to die, but it had never occurred to him that there might have been so many.

He hurried on, passed more blackened skeletons, more scorched paving. Then, something different: another blackened patch of paving, larger than the others. No skeleton lay there, but a pace or so beyond it, a jagged piece of pale gray metal glinted on the street, lying there as though cast aside by some uncaring hand.

Metal calls it, Talith had said. Dammal eyed the pallid shape warily, hurried away from it. Ahead, the ragged spires that might mean safety loomed up higher against the hazy sky.

He was most of the way to the spires when the Gath'talla came for him.

He had a few moments of warning, no more. The hot still air of late afternoon hung heavy over the old street, thick with the rank scent of jungle flowers. Nothing moved—and then all at once birds burst into the air from somewhere nearby, screeching their panic. He turned toward the sound, caught the lightning-scent.

An instant later a blue-white flash lit the trees from beneath, and a sound like sizzling fat came with the light. Dammal blanched, considered running toward the spires, but the stories said the Gath'talla ran swift enough to chase down even a good runner, and turning to run meant giving up any chance of fighting it. He looked around, saw a dark gap in a ruined building nearby, an ancient door not yet covered with vines or filled with rain-washed soil. Would such a thing shelter him? None of the stories mentioned that. He hefted his makeshift spear, decided to face the Gath'talla instead.

Another flash lit the trees, closer. Another crackling sound followed it. Dammal braced himself, drew back the spear.

Then the Gath'talla came out from under the trees.

Its body was like mist or cloud, as the stories said: a cloud around which tiny blue-white gleams flickered, like infant lightnings. A hissing surrounded it, like snakes, like rain plunging into river water. If it had eyes or ears or any other senses, he could not see any mark of them, and where its vital places might be, he could not know. Even so, he flung the makeshift spear at the middle of the thing, and watched it as it flew straight and true.

Blue-white, the flash burst from the center of the thing, leaving Dammal's eyes dazed and half blinded. Then a charred and burning shape that he could only just recognize as his spear fell to the ground beyond it, and the Gath'talla surged toward him.

He turned and sprinted for the dark gap in the ruined building. By the time he reached it the hissing was close behind him, and he plunged into the opening, squirmed past a tangle of debris, twisted around so that at least he would see the thing as it killed him.

Blue unsteady light shone into the darkness, making something glint above the door. A strange tingling rushed over Dammal's bare skin, and the hair on his head rose up of itself, streaming out to all sides. He wormed back into the furthest corner of the space, knowing that it would not save him. Soon enough, he told himself, the Gath'talla would follow him into the space, and he would burn as the spear had burned, as all those others had burned.

The Gath'talla did not follow him. After what seemed a long while, the flickering light faded, the tingling went away, and Dammal's hair settled back to its proper place. He crouched there in the darkness for a longer while still, his heart pounding and his breath coming fast, as his thoughts circled aimlessly around the mystery of why it had spared him. Had it done as jungle cats did, and drawn back only so that it could spring on him once he left the place of safety? He did not know, could not know.

It was a stray memory, finally, that gave him the first whisper of understanding. The tingling feeling on his skin, the rising hair—he'd experienced both of those in a smaller way during unseasonably cold days in the dry season, when he'd stroked the ferrets everyone kept in Atal Thrau to keep the rats at bay. He'd felt the curious tingling then, and seen the fine hairs on his forearm rise. His grandparents, when he'd asked them about it, had shrugged. The loremaster in the school for older children, when he'd done the same, had given him a long quelling look and said that such things were for the Knowers alone to think about.

And there was that one evening, after a day so cool that even the young men bundled themselves up in warm robes, when he'd petted the old gray ferret named Oe and then reached incautiously for something, he never could remember what; when he'd seen the tiny blue flash in the darkness of the little room, and felt a stinging pain, as his hand brushed—

Metal.

He glanced up, to the place above the door where something had glinted. His eyes had adjusted well enough to the darkness by then that he could see it, a bar of the same pallid gray metal he'd seen lying in the street earlier, set into a lintel of stone.

Metal calls it, Talith had said. He stared at the pale gleaming shape, and finally the question that mattered took shape in his mind: if metal calls the Gath'talla, why did the Knowers carry iron-shod staffs with them when they entered Tobed Aun?

He could not pry the metal loose from above the door. He tried everything he could think of, and got only bruised hands for his trouble. Finally, frustrated, he sat down on a patch of bare floor and tried to think through what he needed to do. The only other piece of metal he'd seen anywhere in Tobed Aun was the one he'd passed in the street, lying just past the scorched place. If the Gath'talla was waiting outside to spring on him, he was lost, and even if it had gone seeking prey elsewhere, it might see or sense him and chase him down before he could reach the metal. And if he was wrong, and it offered him no help—

He brushed the thoughts from his mind. Staying holed up in the ruin like a rat in its burrow offered no better prospect, he told himself, and moved toward the sunlight.

His heart pounded as he climbed out through the door into the street, but the lightning-smell was gone and so was the hissing that accompanied the Gath'talla. A glance up the street toward the spires, and then the other way, showed no trace of it. He started walking, fast. Every shift in the wind, every bird fluttering overhead caught at his attention, made him wonder: is it the Gath'talla? He hurried on, past one blackened skeleton, another, still another.

In the distance, somewhere behind him, birds suddenly burst into flight, shrieking in fear. Dammal did not let himself look. He broke into a loping run.

Ruin after tumbledown ruin passed by, and the street ran straight before him between the sheltering trees. The sun had moved well to the west by then, casting Dammal's shadow out in front of him. How far had the metal been? He could not be sure.

Birds cried out again, closer. As they fell silent, Dammal heard a distant whisper of sound, like fat sizzling on a fire. Ahead, he caught sight of a ruined building he thought he remembered, and decided to risk a glance back over his shoulder.

There in the distance, scarcely visible, a little cloud veiled with flickerings seemed to hover over the street. He turned from it with a little desperate cry, threw himself forward with all the strength he had.

Blood rushed in his ears, his breath burst hard from his lips, his feet pounded a steady beat on the ancient stone. Ahead, the westering sun gleamed on something small and bright. He dared not glance back, but he knew it was closing on him: a faint hiss detached itself from the murmur and rustle of the jungle, rose slowly to a roar, and the strange tingling began to play across the skin of his back.

The metal gleamed in the street ahead. As his shadow touched it, Dammal dove forward. He landed belly down with hands outstretched, caught the metal, and rolled.

The Gath'talla was nearly upon him. The billowing cloud edged with small lightnings loomed over him, blotting out the distant spires and the western sky. His hair stood on end, the tingling blazed along his skin like fire, but he raised the lump of metal in his hand, brandished it at the thing.

It drew back, hovered in the air, as though uncertain.

Dammal scrambled to his feet, holding the metal out before him. The Gath'talla backed further away, and then all at once surged to one side, trying to come at him from another angle. Instinct took over, and Dammal flung the metal into the middle of the Gath'talla.

Blue-white, the flash dazzled his eyes, and a sound like a thunderclap shook the jungle; a force Dammal did not understand flung him to the ground. Lightning-smell filled the air. Dimly, through the blackness that followed the glare, he thought he saw the little lightnings tumbling apart, the cloud dispersing, but he could not be sure.

Slowly, his eyes recovered and his breathing and pulse settled to a less frantic beat. He pulled himself off the ground, stood. When he could see clearly again, there was no trace of the Gath'talla anywhere around him—but the pavement beneath where it had been was scorched black, as though burnt.

Off past the blackened place, the piece of metal lay where it had fallen. Dammal went to it, reached down, and jerked his hand away, for the thing was as hot as a coal. After a moment, he went to the jungle to one side of the street, cut a length of vine with a sharp rock. It took him only a little fumbling with a stray stick to get the vine around the metal so he could carry it until it cooled, and the vine blackened but did not burn.

Lightning, he thought, the Gath'talla, the thing that comes off a ferret's fur in cool dry weather. Could they somehow be the same thing? Maybe the Knowers could say, maybe—the idea was shocking, but all the more delicious for that— maybe not even they had that lore.

He raised his head, looked off toward the distant spires. If the Sanctuary existed, if the last of the Ancients still dwelt there, he would find them, he was sure of it. If not, he decided, he would find a safe place to sleep through the night, and if Talith was still there, he would make her take back her words. Why that mattered, he could not say, but it mattered.

Afternoon sun blazed down on leaves and weathered stone as Dammal reached the edge of the place where they had left him the day before. Talith was still there, seated on a gray flat rock over to one side. With the sun's heat so fierce, she'd taken off the black Knowers' robe and wore only a knotted cord around her waist, as the women of Atal Thrau did on hot days. Her staff was out of reach, but the moment she saw Dammal she sprang to her feet and faced him.

"You lied to me," Dammal told her.

She said nothing, watched him through narrowed eyes.

"There's no Sanctuary," he went on, "and no Ancients. I searched all evening and all morning, and there's nothing but empty ruins."

Her face twisted. "I know."

"And the Gath'talla—I killed it. Metal doesn't summon it, metal slays it. You lied about that, too."

"I know," she repeated. Then: "You shouldn't have come back here."

That summoned a bitter laugh. "Where else was I supposed to go?"

That seemed to anger her. "Shall I greet you the way the Eldest instructed me, if you came back?' she snapped at him. "Shall I hold out my arms and murmur more lies to you, draw you down to me, and then use this?" One hand darted to where the knotted cord crossed her back, returned holding a wicked little knife with something black smeared on its tip.

"No one returns from Tobed Aun," she said. As though the words had used up her last strength, she let the little knife fall from her hand, and slumped back down onto the flat stone.

"Listen to me, Dammal," she said dully. "I've told you enough lies; this is the truth. Go back into Tobed Aun. There'll be a new Gath'talla once an egg hatches, but that won't happen until after the rains, so you'll be safe. Go back, and each time the path divides, turn to the left. You'll come to a street that leads off to the left of the spires. Follow that and it'll bring you to a causeway across the marshes. Beyond that the Knowers don't go. Beyond that there are other towns and other peoples. Go there, find whatever waits for you there. I'll return and tell the Eldest that you never came back, and if I'm very lucky, I won't be bound to a stone and flung into the river at night." She gestured wearily toward the trail into Tobed Aun. "Go."

Dammal considered her for what seemed like a long time. The thought of other towns and other peoples, places where the Knowers did not go, blazed up in him like new-kindled fire, but another thought contended with it. It occurred to him that until that moment, when he'd brooded over his rejection by the Knowers, he'd never considered what odious duties they might have placed on him if they'd accepted him into their number.

How many others had been commanded to tell the same lies, wield the same poisoned knife?

"Talith," he said then.

She looked up at him.

"I'll go," he told her, "but you don't need to return. You can come with me if you want."

Her gaze did not leave his face. In it he could see a terrible ambivalence, and something else that startled him. Had she watched him as he'd watched her, and wished as he'd done that the Knowers' rules hadn't raised a barrier between them?

After a moment, he held out a hand to her. Without speaking, she nodded, took it, let him help her to her feet. He gestured toward the trail that led into Tobed Aun; she nodded again, went to get her iron-shod staff. The black robe and the little poisoned knife lay on the ground before her, and she regarded them for a moment, then turned and left them lying there. Together, in silence, they started down the half-overgrown trail.

BORN IN THE gritty Navy town of Bremerton, Washington, and raised in the south Seattle suburbs, JOHN MICHAEL GREER began to write as soon as he could hold a pencil. A widely read author and blogger, he has penned more than forty nonfiction books and fourteen novels. He lives in Rhode Island with his wife Sara.

The Chair In The Garden

By Drew Alexander Ross

(Originally Published in the Book Smuggler's Den, March 2020)

I was a child when my father told me stories about the chair in the garden. We would sit side by side on the couch in our living room while I listened to words that transported me to far-away places. I would flinch in terror or cling in awe as stories of amazing adventures unfolded. He promised me that one day I would discover the doorway to these far-away places for myself. I waited a long time for that day to come.

As we sat in our small living room, he would gaze at the painting that hung above our couch and begin his story—always in the same way.

The painting depicted a scene that could have been in a garden of any old English village; but, there was something magical about it. I imagined that it was the backyard of some grand manor. Two columns of stone pillars, six individual posts in all, ran from foreground to background. The stone pillars supported a wooden pergola covered in flowers and thick green vines, which lead the viewer's eyes toward a row of tall green hedges at the back of the garden beyond the stone columns. A gap in the middle of the hedges revealed a distant field.

In the foreground sat an empty canvas chair, lonely beneath a canopy of vines and a scattered ceiling of pink roses. Sunlight entered from the left, illuminating the chair and just enough of the field beyond to pull its viewers near. Canvas cloth stretched over the chair's wooden frame, forming a scooped cloth seat, its red, blue, and yellow stripes, vibrant against a leafy background of bright yellow, dark green and pale rose.

The stories began with the chair: who had abandoned it, why, and what happened to them? My father told me about the times he left the chair when he was a kid and what lay in the field behind the hedges. I waited for the day when I would begin my own fantastic journeys from that chair, as my father had promised.

One day I did.

Grandma and Grandpa were inside the house looking for me. I was supposed to be doing chores, and they were afraid because I was just old enough where I could get myself into trouble by wandering off. But I never went far. I was outside in the back garden per usual, sitting in that chair, waiting for my adventures to begin. Leaning back in the chair with my arms behind my head and my eyes closed, I heard a noise from the meadow beyond the hedges. Without opening my eyes, I tilted my head toward the sound. It could be anything. Then the noise came again, I knew this was something unusual.

Rising quietly from the chair, I crept through the grass toward the gap in the hedge, staying close to the shadows of the pillars. As I drew nearer, the strange sounds seemed to become a voice. Not a human one. I peered through the gap in the hedge. A giant rabbit, the size of a large dog, sensed my presence with a twitch of its ears and turned to me. Its ears glowed a vibrant shade of dazzling green emeralds. Its fur shone like new snow. Then in one long bound, it stood before me. My heart beat loudly in my ears as I stood taller in an attempt to match its height.

"Help me." The rabbit whispered.

The creature shrunk as I stood straighter. It was only a rabbit, after all. My heart slowed, and the foreboding passed as I saw the creature for what it was, a garden bunny. A garden bunny with green ears. I leaned forward to meet its cool gaze, and I sensed my journey was about to begin. It quirked its head.

"Can you help me?"

My first instinct was to jump at the request like my father always did, but something stayed me.

"Why do you need my help?"

The rabbit smiled a buck-toothed grin. A sparkle of saliva dripped off the tip of its teeth, and I looked down at their sharp edges. They could clip a finger as quickly as Grandpa's weed whacker could trim a blade of grass. I smiled back.

Rabbits ate grass, not fingers.

"Vicious dogs attacked my family hole. I barely escaped!" That rabbit looked over its shoulder. Its green ears twitched. "There was a cave-in. I need your help to clear it so I can get to my children."

The rabbit waited patiently for my response. It didn't seem a mighty task, but my mind drifted to the image of a pack of vicious dogs. Jet black hounds growling with froth that sparkled from their blood-red jowls. Maybe the request wasn't a light one.

But I was determined to have my adventure. This and the rabbit's trapped children chased the pack of rabid dogs from my mind.

"I will help," I said. "Show me to your home."

The rabbit bowed its head and hopped back across the meadow. I took a step through the hedges and followed.

The meadow stretched for acres. Deep yellow and green grass swallowed me in. After a while, the grass was all I could see. The grass grew taller the farther we went from the hedges. The rabbit led and popped its head up every ten feet or so to make sure I was still in sight. I kept my eyes on the small burrow in the clumps of low grasses leading me further on my journey.

The long grass gave way to a field of reeds that soaked up the sun and created an oven around my chest and stomach. I crouched low to be closer to the cooler earth, but the potential dangers began to weigh on me in the form of a sweat-soaked shirt. *I wanted this*, I told myself as the skip in my step faded, beaten down by doubts and a strange primitive twinge of uncertainty.

Finally, a hill approached, and I lifted my head to breathe in an invigorating gust of wind and wide-open space. My mouth gaped as I took in the colorful wonders surrounding me, and I questioned whether I was still asleep, dreaming in the canvas chair.

A forest flanked the side of the reed field and went into the distance toward the meadows of grass. Trees with lime green, canary yellow, and lagoon blue leaves watched over the fields. There was a darker line on the horizon, and I wondered what mysteries these lands held. We had to be close to the rabbit's hole, though. I bent down and spotted the ruffle in the short grass ahead of me.

"Mr. Rabbit!" I called.

One green ear poked out of the low grass, followed by its little head.

"Is your hole in the forest?"

"Are we near the forest?"

"No. It's off a ways."

"Keep your head down when we pass!" The rabbit said. "That's where the dogs live."

Before I could nod, the rabbit dove back into its tunnel, and the ruffle of low grass moved on ahead. I frowned and resumed my pace, cursing myself for not asking more questions. At this rate, it would be dark before I got back to the house. I didn't want to think about Grandpa's reaction to that. My tongue swelled, and the back of my neck burned. I raised my head and inhaled deeply to catch one more reviving breeze before I put my head back down on the trail.

I kept my ears pricked, hearing the chirps of exotic birds. I scanned the drunks of the forest looking for any sign of the animals but kept one eye out for any sign of a vicious beast. Only the glittering forest beckoned, and I moved on, captivated.

My ease was stifled suddenly when a roar pierced through the fields and left a ringing in my ears. My eyes searched for the source of the cry, and I saw a much larger bulge in the long grass a little ways off. A splinter of pain pierced my toe.

Ducking down, I saw the rabbit release the big toe of my shoe with a drip of my blood trailing from its teeth. The rabbit glowed and began to pulsate. It began to grow, and its ears shined dark before the rabbit caught its breath.

"That's the cry of the beast!" The rabbit said.

"The creature sounded in pain."

"It caught our scent. It's trying to lure you into a trap!"

I didn't know what to say to this. I watched the rabbit tremble. My toe throbbed. What would it feel like if the beast bit me?

I was scared, but I wanted to see another creature in this land. If rabbits had green ears and could grow in size, I wanted to see what other animals here were like. A glimpse of the dog might be worth it. I looked back at the rabbit. Its eyes bulged, and its nose flared. I decided not to give the rabbit an option.

"I'm going to take a look."

"Hurry back." The rabbit bristled. "And don't get too close!"

I crouched low through the stalks. I couldn't see where I was going, so I headed toward the direction of the last wail. Slowly, I rose up and arched my neck to peek over the reeds. A loud wail echoed, and I jerked my head down. The creature was a few yards away.

I crept forward.

A gap in the stalks revealed a wolf-like creature with two sparkling, bright blue eyes. Its fur was glossy with a sheen of charcoal black and had a tail almost as wide as its body, like a beaver's. The tail, the color of topaz, was soaked in fresh blood. My eyes wavered at the sight, and that's when I noticed the thorns wedged into its tail. The blood dripping from the creature was its own. It roared again.

I looked closer and thought that this creature was too regal to be one of those vicious dogs the rabbit feared. Even in its pain, it looked majestic. My body shot upright to enter the clearing when I saw the wolf lean to its tail and attempt to bite the thorns loose.

The creature looked up toward me and emitted a low growl. Its tail rose and resembled a club waiting to be swung. I held up my hands and stared into its blue eyes. It looked back at me and sniffed the air.

I took a few slow steps forward.

"I can remove the thorns."

Its tail, resembling a powerful club, twitched as it thought.

I held out my hand to allow the creature to take my scent and judge my character. Though my hand shook, I stood as tall as I could. It bent forward and lowered its snout. It could have devoured my arm with one snap of its jaw, but instead, it turned and lowered its tail.

I let out a pent up breath, then moved to the tail to inspect the damage. The thorns were deep and caked in a mix of fresh and dry blood.

My heart beat in rhythm with my Adam's apple as my hands moved over its tail. My ears felt the pulse of blood rushing to my head, and I tensed at any sharp intake of breath from the wolf. Though time seemed to slow in those tense few minutes, I was able to remove the thorns with great care. I finished, and the wolf licked its tail and swung it through the air with satisfaction.

"How did you injure your tail?"

The creature turned to me.

"I was hunting. My enemy has terrorized the innocent for too long." It said. "But the evil creature protected its lair with thorns and escaped while I was left to lick my wounds."

The wolf surveyed me for a moment and finally approached.

"Thank you." It murmured.

It licked my face and turned away. It was then that the wolf resembled a dog. I remembered the rabbit's warnings, and my eyes dropped to the ground.

"I have to go," I said. "Another creature needs my help."

The wolf nodded.

"Like father, like son."

My head quirked at the words, but I just stared as the creature trotted back toward the woods.

"Make sure you're back through the hedges before nightfall. The powers of evil grow in the dark."

The wolf disappeared into the woods, and I hurried back through the reeds, trying to remember if my father told me a story about this wolf.

The sun crept lower in the sky, and the heat began to dwindle. I didn't have time to reflect on sentiments. I relished the more refreshing breezes that came with the dying sun, but I quickened my steps. When I found the rabbit, it was frantically hopping about.

"I thought I lost you!" The rabbit exclaimed.

"I'm alright. A creature was in pain, and I helped. I hurried back as fast as I could."

"We should be moving. It's not safe to be here for too long."

"Will I have time to get back to my house before dark?" I asked.

"If we don't waste any more time."

We moved on to the dark area on the horizon. It was marked by a line of decaying trees. Neither vibrancy nor color existed in this world within a world. The only sign of life were the footprints of a seemingly large animal etched into the muddy ground. Dirt and mud caked the land, and the footprints of a large animal marked the territory. The rabbit did not speak as it moved further into the dark territory.

Snap.

A dead branch cracked from somewhere behind me. I turned and thought I saw a shadow dart across the edge of my vision.

"We are close," the rabbit said. "We must hurry."

I expected the rabbit would be alert to any danger if its family was in potential harm, but he pounced ahead fearlessly with vigor. I wanted to finish my adventure. I wanted to return to Grandpa and Grandma, who were bound to be ill with worry over my absence. The feelings of guilt were repressed quickly as I thought of the rabbit's family in danger, which reminded me of my mission. I moved on.

The rabbit bounded ahead and turned behind a mound of upturned earth by the roots of a gigantic tree: the rabbit hole. Its home. We finally reached our destination. I walked over and inspected the hole. It was just wide enough for me to fit in.

The rabbit seemed to be bigger again. And now, its white fur was the grey slush of old snow. It stared at me, its eyes hollow. I wondered if the creature thought it was too late to save its family.

"What can I do?"

The rabbit licked its lips.

"I'm too small to break down the packed earth at the cave in. It would take me too long to get through to my family with my claws and teeth. I'm worried they're starving already."

"How can I help?"

The rabbit licked its lips.

"Use your size down in the hole. Your strength will break through." The rabbit said. "I'll wait behind you to scoop out the leftover earth."

I nodded and made my way into the mouth of the hole.

On hands and knees, I crawled into the dark, confined space. I could crouch, but the faint light from the sun gave me limited visibility. My breath grew heavy. The earth was cold, and I felt a shiver crawl up my spine where my sweat chilled. I did not want to stay in this space long.

I reached the cave-in and dug at the dirt barrier. My hands clawed at the packed earth, but there wasn't any give to the ground. Sweat poured down my face while the coldness of the tunnel made my shirt clam up against my back. I longed for more of the earlier, blazing sun.

Frustrated, I jabbed a fist at the earth, and my hand sparked with pain. I jerked back. Blood trickled down my palm in a steady flow. I squished to one side so I could let the light from the mouth of the tunnel illuminate my hand. It was a small puncture. I moved a little more. *What caused this?*

My shoulder brushed against the side of the cave, and more sparks of pain pierced my side. I held in a yelp and turned more carefully to let light in.

Thorns.

My heart jumped in my throat. I began to feel claustrophobic as I noticed vines of a thorn bush curls along the sides and ceiling of the tunnel. It felt like a rock replaced my Adam's apple. I struggled to inhale shallow breaths filled with terror.

In panic, I turned to the mouth of the cave, but the last light of the day was suddenly blocked off. I thought back to the sound of the snapped branch as we entered this dead woods.

A green glow filled the tunnel. I had to blink my eyes to focus my vision.

When my vision cleared, I wished light hadn't returned. The creature I thought was a garden bunny filled the cave with its bulk. Its green ears illuminated the cave with a poisonous neon light, creating a deathly grey hue over its fur, which stood on end. Its teeth now seemed like they could take off my arm as easily as my fingers. Its eyes reflected a soulless pit.

"Finally!" The creature cackled. "I waited for your father to come back for years! I don't mind settling for the son."

I couldn't make a sound. I was too paralyzed to even whimper. The rabbit swayed from side to side, and I realized there was nowhere for me to go.

I knew I couldn't win, but I couldn't let my last moments be in fear. I set myself to make whatever stand I could and got to my feet. I shut my eyes and ran forward in a fumbling crouch.

At the last second, I opened my eyes to see if I would make contact. The rabbit's claws flashed toward my face. I turned and felt thorns tear into my shoulder. I stumbled and dove before it could strike again. My uninjured shoulder collided with the rabbit, knocking us both off our feet.

I scrambled to see the rabbit was ready for another strike.

I steadied my footing in a low crouch. The upward curve of the ground showed the entrance was just ahead. I fixed my eyes on the fading light at the mouth of the tunnel and hoped that one more shove, or maybe a lucky dodge, would give me a chance at freedom.

The monster blocked my way.

It lunged for me, and I sprang to the side of the tunnel. More thorns pierced my back. The rabbit turned to face me. Its teeth opened wide, and I dove back down the hole. I was so close to the opening, but there was nowhere else I could turn. I shuddered at the ferocious growls echoing towards me.

When I turned back to face the rabbit, I saw it readying itself to pounce. Its claws worked furiously against the ground. Its ears began to pulsate their sickening green light, which skewed my vision. With squinted eyes, I watched the evil green and grey blob pounce for me as I attempted to make one last run for the entrance. Its paws brought me to the ground.

Claws sank into my chest. I let out a

yell of pain and despair. I flipped over, refusing to let the rabbit look into my eyes as it finished the job. I prepared in that brief moment for the inevitable sharp plunge into my neck and the total darkness that would follow.

But something was wrong.

Its teeth missed my neck and plunged straight into the dirt. I let out a furious, wavering roar as I scrambled maniacally for my life toward the exit. I had utterly forgotten the mysterious shadow that snapped the branch from before.

The shadow moved across the opening, and light filled my vision. The wolf! Blood dripped from its teeth. I turned at the mouth of the cave as it moved to let me out and saw the haunch of the rabbit punctured with bloody holes.

The rabbit turned and met my gaze. Its mouth trembled with foam. It pounced forward and leaped toward me.

CRUNCH!

The wolf's massive tail swung down and entombed the mouth of the cave with dirt. A ferocious snarl was muted by fallen earth. The wolf made the final touches to entomb the evil rabbit in its hole, forever.

I turned and saw the wolf pant. The setting sun cast a golden background against its black sheen. It looked back at the sun and turned to me.

"We must get you home." It panted. "Hop on my back."

Still in shock, I hurried to obey. I jumped on its back, and we were off. The wolf's paws tore up the earth as we raced through the decrepit branches and the looming, lifeless trees. As the wind of the oncoming nightfall brushed our backs, we burst into the field of reeds to race the setting sun. Deer with purple antlers and birds with transparent wings watched our dash across the fields.

There was a sliver of light left as the wolf passed through the meadow and approached the hedges. It stopped at the barrier. I hopped off its back and turned to the wolf.

"How can I ever thank you?" My head hung.

The wolf brought its snout under my chin and raised it high.

"You helped me with the thorns." It replied. "And I damaged the rabbit's lair. He tricked you by twisting a story of my own effort to stop him."

"I was gullible."

"Those who prey on others with the guise of the weak are the most cunning of all. You acted from the goodness of your heart. There is never shame in that."

"I was scared." My head dropped.

"You stood true in the end."

I picked my head up.

"Don't let anything shake your resolve to help others, little one."

The sun began to creep out of sight.

"You must go now."

I smiled and hugged the wolf.

"I have one question."

Its head twitched.

"What did you mean like, 'like father like son?'"

"Your father came here a long time ago. I recognized your scent." The wolf stated. "He said one day his son would come to this land."

The wolf grinned.

I smiled in return, and we both turned our separate ways. The wolf went back into the meadow. I ran back through the hedges and collapsed into the chair in the garden.

I looked down from the painting and squeezed the shoulders of my wide-eyed son curled up next to me. Earlier, he had crept down the stairs well past his bedtime. Not unlike the many nights I did when I was his age.

He took a seat next to me on the couch and looked up at the painting. He asked about who left that empty chair. Where did they go? I looked up at the painting and began to tell him my first adventure with the chair in the garden.

DREW ALEXANDER ROSS studied business and film at the University of San Francisco, class of 2015. He resides in Los Angeles, where he worked in education and currently makes a living freelancing. Drew's primary focus is screenwriting, and he enjoys reading a book a week across various genres, fantasy foremost. He has placed in three screenwriting competitions and has short stories featured in several publications.

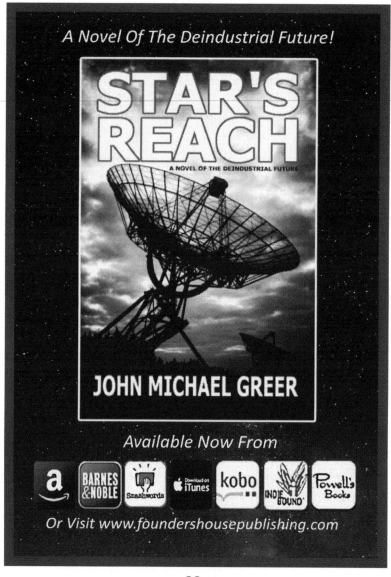

The 'aiei of Snow

By D.A. D'Amico

(Originally appeared in Electric Spec Magazine: February 2017)

The snowstorm crawled down from the mountain with a force I hadn't seen in many years. I shuddered as flakes struck my parched lips, tasting the world as it had been seventy winters earlier. It was the world of my father, the time when I first discovered the power of magic, and the nature of loss.

Little Achlie, son of my son Piath, crouched beside me. His dark eyes shone wet and glassy. He'd been crying.

"It tastes bitter," he sobbed. "It tastes. . . sad."

"I nodded, remembering the first time I'd tasted the *'aiei* that makes the world.

I'd been eight, a slight boy for my age. My father sat with his back to the village, a sliver of steel held tightly across his lap. I didn't let him see I'd been crying as I threw myself silently onto the wide log beside him, but he knew anyway.

"What troubles you?" His wrinkled, nut-brown face was solemn as he caught my eye, as if to tell me this would be a conversation between two men, and not father and son. It was the first time he'd treated me as an equal, and shame colored my cheeks. Grown men didn't cry about childish things.

I hesitated, unsure the problems appearing so large to my young mind would even be worth his notice. The way he viewed me was every bit as important as how I viewed myself. Did I really wish to risk losing his respect over a beating and a game of find the seeker?

"A boy accused me of cheating," I blurted out suddenly, my eyes afraid to meet his. Instead, I watched his strong hands as he smashed a delicate shaft of iron against a rasp of blackened steel. A curl of metal peeled away, falling into the small pile already littering the pine needles at his feet. Then he struck again, teasing the shapeless iron into a fine point.

My father had taken up the hammer and become my people's smith only two summers earlier. The old iron master had fallen ill, dying quickly. Most in the village were sure my father hadn't the time necessary to learn the techniques, but he'd excelled, rapidly achieving the old master's level of competence. It was as if my father had somehow known the man would die.

"But you didn't?" His hands momentarily stopped their filing to brush fine grey powder from his leather apron. "You just *knew* where the boy had hidden himself?"

His insight startled me. It was as if he'd prepared for this conversation even before I'd dumped my small frame onto the log beside him.

He sighed, setting his tools aside, rising slowly to his feet among a shower of metal shavings and exclamations at growing old, and draped the leather swatch onto the worn patch of log where he'd been sitting.

"Tell me what you see, Tokori?" He used the nickname I'd acquired as a baby because of my wide-eyed owlish stare of wonder at the world. It was an elfish word, and as such it held a measure of wonder in itself. I knew he meant to put me at ease, but his concern made me feel as if I were somehow smaller. I was no longer a man in his eyes. I was the owl boy, Tokori. "What do you see around you?"

Scattered birches thrust yellowed fingers into a sky so blue it was as if the ocean had been painted overhead. Maples flared with the last fires of their summer lives, and fitful shadows chased soft breezes across the tall grass like invisible rabbits playing.

Beauty filled the landscape to bursting, but typical of all boys everywhere I ignored the wonders around me and replied merely, "Trees."

He sounded displeased, as if I'd failed some test. "Open your eyes. See the life that's inside everything, from the worms under the dirt, to the eagles high in the heavens. The *'aiei* of creation fills the air like thick smoke."

'aiei was for children, for bedtime stories around the fire. The elves had taken the *'aiei* with them when men forced them from the world. It was nothing but a word now, having no substance. In those days, I was both too old and too young for magic.

I shrugged. A flush of warmth crossed my features. "I'm sorry, father. I don't know what you expect from me."

He glanced down. His small dark eyes shone like freshly chipped flint, hard and penetrating. I felt him peering through me, searching beneath my skin to spy out the secrets of my soul.

"What were you doing when you first realized where the other boys were hiding?" He asked finally, looking away, releasing me from the crushing weight of his stare.

Already, it seemed foolish to have come whining to my father over it. I'd joined a group of older boys who'd been released from their morning chores, and together we played a game of hunting and seeking. One boy would be chosen to track, to flush the others from their roosts, perches, burrows, or dens. It was a game I'd played many times, enjoying the hunt, delighting in the pleasure of predator versus prey.

Ishki, a boy three summers older than I, tall and strong and already growing hair in places that marked him as a man, had challenged me. He claimed the ability to evade any seeker; having both a superior den in which to hide, as well as a foolproof manner of escape should he be found out. Ever boastful, in the ways of all boys, I said I could find him easily. I hadn't really believed it, but boys have trouble keeping their mouths shut at any age. He dared me in front of others, and I couldn't refuse. So, I closed my eyes, leaning into the moss-covered trunk of a great maple, and began to count.

As my face pressed against the tepid dampness of the woody moss, I *knew*. I could *taste* the boy's secret. I even touched my tongue to the moist cushion of bark, feeling the cool beads of trapped stagnant water clinging within the fibrous strands. The image of Ishki's hiding place was like a drawing in colored liquids, a moment in time, almost frozen, oozing like honey through my mind.

"It was beneath the unmarried woman's longhouse," I said as I told my father the tale. "It was as plain to me as the sun sparkling on that ribbon of stream over there. So I cornered him."

"Did he escape?"

"No," I said. "I'd asked Mikala to pretend to find the front of his hole, and she enlisted a group of the women to shout curses and describe what they would do to any man unlucky or stupid enough to be in such a place."

My father smiled a little when I mentioned Mikala. He hadn't thought I liked her, and I didn't really, not then, but she would be my wife by arrangement in the coming years.

"And you were waiting for him as he emerged from his hiding place?"

"I tapped him the moment his head became visible above the bend in the reeds concealing his tunnel. He shrieked like an infant. I suppose he thought I was one of the unmarried women, come to do the horrible things they'd promised."

My father nodded gravely. "We can-not fault him for his fear of angry women. I would not want to tangle with such creatures myself."

He said it with such a straight face that I burst out laughing. He did the same soon after, unable to keep his composure. I felt suddenly warm inside. We'd shared a moment only two men could share.

He sobered, one last chuckle escaping his thin, dark lips. "Then he beat you?"

I nodded. "Him, and Tollok, and Knon."

"You fought back?"

I gave him a withering look. It was an expression of disapproval I wouldn't have used on my father before that day.

"I did not mean offense, my son," he said. "You've clearly been in a fight."

I peered down. My rough, woven-grass tunic was torn and matted with mud. My upper lip and right temple throbbed, bruised and tender.

"Follow me," he said.

We walked to the muddy edge of the stream in silence. My father bent, searching the moist gravel. His long fingers darted over small pebbles, pressing some with hesitation, as if expecting them to come alive under his touch. Finally, he selected two, clutching one in each hand.

"Take this one." He handed me the rounded, black lump. It felt dry and warm in my palm.

"What do you feel?" My father asked.

I told him I felt like throwing it in the water just to see it splash. He smiled.

25

"That only means you're a boy."

He handed me the other stone. It glistened with moisture, still wet from the riverbank. I stared at it, finding no urge to throw it away. Instead, I raised it to my lips and tasted it.

The moment the pebble touched my tongue I gasped in surprise. It felt cold, far colder than it should have. I glanced up. The sky was gone, replaced by an arching expanse of grey ice shot through with veins of light blue the color of a robin's egg. I couldn't breathe. The ice crushed me, suffocating and endless.

Then I blinked, and it vanished.

My father hadn't moved. The stream still gurgled, rushing on its indirect path to the south, sunlit and warm. Breezes still tossed clusters of reeds back and forth in a slow dance, shaking the ochre carpet into animation. The vision had been so vivid, so powerful, that I suddenly believed my childish fears and superstitions.

"What did you do?" I trembled in the remembered chill.

"I merely handed you two pebbles. What happened after came from within you?"

"What *did* happen?"

"*'aiei,*" he said. "What the elves called magic."

"Is there really magic in the rocks?" I fought for breath, not really comprehending. I'd taken so much of his stories as fantasy.

"The rocks hold a share," he said. "But living things possess greater potential."

He knelt, sitting on his haunches. I did the same, expecting a long explanation. I thought magic was just a story for the very young, or comfort for the very old. I thought it no longer existed. I'd been wrong.

"If *'aiei* still fills all things, then how is it I only know of it from songs and fairytales?"

"The gift is rare. Only a few can sense the *'aiei* of existence," he said. "It may be we have a touch of the *folk* in us. Your grandfather could hear the wind whispering the thoughts of eagles. The breezes spoke to him, and told him when the rain would come, or when a herd of elk might follow the paths near the winter lodge.

"My gift is more modest. I see the inner lives of the stones. I feel their desires." He glanced at me as he spoke, expecting me to laugh. I might have, had I not felt the *'aiei* for myself, sensed its depth and power.

This revelation frightened me. How would being able to manipulate the waters help me as I made my way through life? Would it find food for my family? Could I take it to Faulindium, the great walled city on the eastern shore, and become a knight?

I asked my father these things.

"I don't know." His eyes took on a faraway look, as if he saw something I couldn't.

"When the stones told me Timon the iron master would die, and that I must continue his work, I wavered. It wasn't my desire. Why should I obey the *'aiei?* Then a vision came, the first and only I've ever had. I not only saw, but felt, our village dying. Our numbers grew thin with hunger and disease. Your mother lay dead, discarded like rubbish in the snow, her eyes sunken and dull."

I fidgeted at the thought of harm coming to my mother. He noticed my distress, nodding in understanding. Then he put an arm around my shoulders and pulled me close.

"I picked up the blacksmith's hammer the very next day," he said. "The rocks guided my hands, instructing me in ways Timon never could. I can squeeze steel from stone like water from a sponge. I shape it according to its whim, listening all the while as it takes my hands where it will."

At that moment, I finally understood my father. His quiet patience and resigned sense of purpose stilled me. A pebble of shining metal had decided his life. He'd become a slave to rocks for the sake of his family. I loved him more deeply for that.

He leaned forward, dipping his right hand into the fast-flowing water at the edge of the stream.

"I can hear a thousand whispers in the sand carried by this water," my father said. "Each voice is a song, poetry, a chorus of history. If I concentrate, I can make out individual tones."

He shook his head as if clearing his mind of voices only he could hear.

"And you? What does the water tell you, my son?"

Nervously, I reached in and brought a handful of cold, clear water to my lips. It had the slight tang river water gets near the end of summer when the leaves begin dying, but otherwise, I tasted nothing.

"This stream is born in the mountains far to the north, in the land once inhabited by giants." My father's gaze met mine as he continued to speak.

"It meets many other rivers as it finds its way to the forest where the colossal redwoods grow and the dwarves used to play. It travels further than any man can walk, and with it comes the 'aiei of the earth, the wind, and all living things. When you are ready, my son, you will see this."

"But not now?"

"No." He turned away. "The magic is new to you, and it will come and go as it pleases."

I dipped my fingers once more. The icy chill crawled up my arm, and with it the sensation of movement. The gravel bottom seemed to recede, and I slid beneath the waters. I screamed. Frigid liquid burned my throat, and I saw my father beneath me, sinking into the black depths. I fell back, and found myself on shore once more.

"Another vision?" My father stood beside me, concern on his features.

I gasped, my heart pounding. "No, nothing."

I did not want him to know I'd seen his death.

I smelled the rain hanging on the air like coarsely ground pepper, spicy and invasive. My father told me it was neneki, the smell lightning makes as it slashes its way through the cloudy sky, but I knew it wasn't. Lightning smelled flat and metallic. This was something very different. It had range and depth. The rain's odor held a thousand different moments all tumbled together.

"'aiei," I whispered, remembering our conversation by the stream a few weeks earlier. I'd put the final prophetic vision of his death from my mind by then, pretending it had never happened.

My father glanced up from the thin strip of black iron he'd been polishing with a rough leather cloth, and flicked his head in the direction of the bachelor's house. I understood, saying nothing more about magic. Instead, I spoke of my excitement. We'd be hunting together soon.

He smiled warmly, cinching both the cloth and the metal around a wooden shaft held tightly between his bare knees. A thin, naked boy younger than myself, his arms, face, and chest smeared with ash and pitch, jumped forward. My father held out the stick, and the boy clutched it against his small body as if he'd just been given a great gift.

"This will need the hot resin, just like I showed you, Moahb," my father instructed the boy. "I will check it when I return."

He ran a hand through Moahb's shaggy hair, giving him a playful tap on the behind as the boy scrambled away. I felt jealous at the way my father treated his apprentice. They spent much time together, sharing stories and making memories forever hidden from me. My father treated him as a son, and I both envied and resented that bond.

"Will we go now?" I asked, perhaps a bit too loudly. I was eager to separate my father from my rival.

"The first rule of a hunter is patience, my son," he said. Then he laughed when he noticed my stricken look. "Come."

I leapt from my crouch on the woven reed mat carpeting the entrance to the blacksmith's house, and snatched my leather sack. It contained dried fish wrapped in oiled leaves, tinder and flint for making fire, and a small bladder full of drinking water.

We laughed as we trekked through the forest, kicking through drifts of leaves the color of the setting sun. Clouds rolled in, quickly darkening the sky as we made our way from the edge of the valley up into the hills. Timidly, it started to rain in soft droplets that beaded and trickled off our grease-smeared jerkins.

My father told tales as we marched. His stories were invariably of the *eidder days*, and they portrayed great adventures involving magical creatures. He chronicled the races of men who were not human, and gave fanciful accounts of the power of *'aiei*. These stories were from a time long before the days of his father's father, he'd said.

One tale involved the expulsion of the elves, and how a single champion had bested their mighty armies. I listened attentively. These would be the stories I'd tell my own children, and they to their grandchildren.

Finally, my father pointed to an overhanging lump of lichen-covered granite, and I dropped my pack onto the relative dryness beneath. We ate cold fish and nuts in companionable silence, each lost in our own thoughts. My father seemed happier than he'd been for a long time. Part of me knew it was the hunt, but inside I liked to think his happiness stemmed from the bond we were forming, the time we'd share.

We didn't try to light a fire that night. The wind had increased, sending intermittent gusts into our cleft, and any attempt at a flame would surely have led to failure. We slept within a crook of rock that looked as if it'd been split by a giant axe, cleaved neatly into two sections. My father held me as we huddled in the darkness, sharing our warmth.

Outside, the rain fell like spittle from an old woman's lips, fitfully, in great gobs, and then suddenly switching to miniscule sprays and jets of icy fluid. It was still one of the happiest times I could remember.

I awoke once in the middle of the night with an intense feeling of dread, thinking I heard voices. Soft murmurs sang to me as I struggled against slumber, gurgling with the patter of the rain. I turned to my father, but he'd vanished.

In my dream, I stepped into darkness. Unease carried me down into the channel cut by a slow-moving stream. I could see nothing.

"Father?" My teeth chattered from the cold as my nervousness increased. Above me, the rain ignited individual drops, and they glowed with a faint blue luminescence. The stream dribbled like tar at my feet. My breath came in ragged sobs as I fell in the mud, knowing what I'd find.

My father lay face down in the frigid water. His prone body cast no shadow in the wan cobalt light. I howled as I pulled him onto the bank, his body stiff, his eyes clouded and dull. The water boiled where it touched me, fleeing from my pain as I struggled to hold my father close. The stream exploded. Rain pressed down in torrents as my anguish fueled the maelstrom. Waves tore over the rocks beside me, breaking in churning sheets. A whirlpool formed a cocoon around my father's lifeless body. Cherry red sparks ripped through the azure glow, landing like hot ash on my father's forehead, congealing against his pale skin. It covered his face like a mask.

"Please don't leave me!" I shrieked at the body, attempting by sheer volume to move him. His lips bubbled, mimicking my words.

His body twitched. Cold fingers grasped me, and I collapsed.

When I awoke, the sun had risen. The clouded sky churned, restless and animated, the color of ashes from a dead campfire. My father perched on a boulder nearby. He shifted when I opened my eyes.

"You slept poorly, little Tokori. Does the magic haunt you?" His tight features appeared fluid. His dark face rippled. My distress must have been visible, because he climbed down and sat beside me in the sand. A patina of sweat covered his naked body, although a cool breeze churned from the mountains.

"I thought you were dead." I tried to keep my voice neutral, but memories of the previous night caused me to falter. The air seemed to thicken. Something inside me screamed it was true. He *would* die. Soon.

I stared at him, hoping for a release from my nightmare. None came. I could read the answer in his eyes, once flinty and dark, now watery blue. I licked my lips, my mouth suddenly dry. I wanted to cry, but the tears wouldn't come. Tightness in my chest tugged me forward into his arms. His touch chilled me, and I had a vision of stars, endless, bleak darkness. When I pulled back, it was as if a piece of my soul still clung to him.

"We all die. It's the way of things." He caressed me, his fingers burning where they touched.

"No!" I scrambled away, my chest heaving, my breath exploding from my lips like steam.

He hesitated. Anguish made his face sag. His shoulders slumped, and he seemed to melt as he turned from me.

We sat that way through most of the bleak morning. I felt lost in troubled thoughts, my father within an arm's reach of me, but already gone. The 'aiei seemed more a curse now than ever.

"Magic can feel like a cruel master," he whispered as if reading my thoughts. "But it has the power to transcend this time, and this world."

"I don't understand."

"You will." He tussled my hair, and it was as if he shook the troubling thoughts from my head.

The grey sky churned, restless and animated, the color of ashes from a dead campfire. My heart had lightened. My father seemed more alive than I could ever remember, his step nimble, his eyes sharp as we stalked a red fox through the heavy blanket of leaves.

We'd spotted the animal's scat by an unused trail not far from where we'd spent our night. The dung smelled pungent and acidic, with overtones of acorns. The odor was a clear sign it had been deposited very recently, so the ani-mal was still nearby.

We scouted for traces, and found them a short distance to the north. I crept up on the animal's den from down-wind, deliberately sowing my scent and a fair amount of noise. My father waited with a bow and a single slender arrow tipped with black steel.

"Come on out!" I cupped my hands, hollering and thumping the earth with my feet.

The fox, as if obeying my com-mand, flew from its borough and direct-ly across my father's path. My father struck. The arrow arced from his bow. The fox seemed to hesitate. Its small, cinnamon-colored ears twitched. Its body shivered. Then it reversed direc-tion, hopping up to meet the deadly pro-jectile.

And it died.

My father reached it first. The arrow had caught the creature beneath its fore-limbs, killing it quickly, painting its fur in a brighter shade of crimson.

"You didn't aim correctly." I kneeled down beside him. "If the fox hadn't veered, you would've missed."

"The steel whispered to me in the fi-nal moment," he said softly. "I listened."

"'aiei?" I asked as if the forest had ears.

"'aiei." He nodded.

"Speaking about magic as if it were a normal part of the world is unsettling," I said. "I don't know if I can get used to it."

"It was the same for me at your age." He began to dress the kill. His fingers dipped deeply into the pelt, and then he hesitated.

"There's much of the earth in all

living things. Your grandfather spoke about the *'aiei* in life's very breath." My father tapped his chest. "He could comprehend the wind inside a body."

"I can feel the pull of muscles and bone, the whisper of iron within the blood," he continued. "It's a powerful sensation when felt through the newly killed. The *'aiei* of life is strong, very strong."

He held the pelt open, exposing raw flesh and bright organs. He told me to dip my finger in the blood. I did. Then he told me to taste it. I hesitated. Then, slowly, I brought my finger up and touched it to my tongue.

... I push through a small hole smelling of dirt and musty leaves, a rat's plump, warm body somewhere just ahead. My fur bristles and contracts, letting me feel the tunnel walls as I race ahead. My snout twitches, and I smell the delicious stench of terror coming from the darkness...

...I'm rolling on my back. The tall grass caresses my fur as the bright sunshine warms my belly. Suddenly, a shadow cuts across the sun, and my brothers are on top of me. The pile shifts from one to the other as we play and roll across the verdant hillside...

...I'm bounding through an endless field of poppies, my ears just tickling the pollen-laden bulbs. Up ahead I smell her. She's ready, signaling with a yipping pant that means she knows I'm approaching...

I felt as if it had lasted for years, but when the impressions ceased, my father had not moved, his fingers still wet with blood. The rain had started again, light flecks against my cheeks to hide my tears. I felt sick.

I felt the same as when I'd dreamt of my father's death.

"I'll never hunt fox again!" I cried. "I'll never hunt anything."

"That will pass," my father said. "The *'aiei* of blood is too strong, but it will fade as all things must."

And it did grow fainter. The unbearable emotions passed, dribbling from my mind like warm water through my fingers. I was able to eat some of the meat my father had roasted on skewers, chewing the tender chunks slowly and deliberately as if they were made of thick leather. My soul remained disturbed, rebelling.

"Is this a curse? Did the elves leave their *'aiei* behind to punish us?" My thoughts spilled out as we sat quietly by the fire.

"Magic existed long before the war, long before the folk were defeated and sent to whatever realm they now occupy."

"But I thought *they* were the magical ones," I said. "All the stories, all the songs, say elfish magic could move mountains and draw the stars to the ground."

"What the elves did with the *'aiei* made them different," he said. "Yes, they could bend it to their will and make it obey, but the *'aiei* belongs to all things."

I tossed a twig into the fire, watching the sparks dance as they climbed into the heavens. It reminded me of a very old song recounting the day of defeat, the *eidder day*, when the elves were banished from the world of men.

Flames gone all wrong
Seeds scattered in storm

They vanish on high
Like sparks against the sky

"So, men cannot command the 'aiei?"

My father nodded. "Magic has its own business in this world. We interact with it, but only on terms it dictates. It's not for us to know more."

"But what good is it?"

"'*aiei* brought me to the iron. Without that...."

Without a blacksmith, there'd be no new blades. The hunters would be forced to craft cruder versions for themselves, losing time, losing advantage. The village would grow hungry and die, as in my father's vision.

"Will the magic demand I take up the hammer and anvil?" I asked, selfish in my youth. I didn't want to give up the thrill of the chase, or the exhilaration that comes from the hunt. I wanted to travel, to see the great cities by the shore. I wanted to meet royalty, to see the spires of the rose-colored castle where the queen held court and men from lands I've never even dreamt of paid homage. My village was home. It was all I've ever known, but still, I wanted more.

I remembered my father's face as we stalked the fox, the glint of pure joy in his dark eyes. I hadn't seen him that happy since he first struck steel, and somehow, I knew I'd never see him that happy again. The knowledge felt like a boulder on my chest.

"No," my father replied. "That's why I teach little Moahb to carry the hammer. The '*aiei* has greater things in mind for you."

I frowned at the mention of my fa-ther's apprentice. He chuckled, reaching over to stroke my hair.

"Fear not," he laughed. "I will always have just one son, my little Tokori. Remember, I will always love you. The magic links us. I will always be with you in the 'aiei."

With that, he would speak no more. He put his arm around me and we sat watching the fire until darkness came. We slept under the sky, warmed by the glowing coals. The clouds parted sometime during the night, revealing a multitude of stars so sharp they almost seemed within reach.

I had no further dreams of his death.

An icy spray fell from the sky a few days after I'd returned from the hunting trip. The rain struck me intermittently with needle sharp jabs as I helped haul woven grass baskets of pecans and walnuts from the village houses to winter storage. It was work for all. I participated gladly, happy to be with my friends.

Ishki, the boy who'd beaten me some weeks earlier but who was now my friend, stood beside me. Mikala, my someday wife, crouched between us. The way Ishki stared at the girl made me uneasy, and I felt we might not remain friends for very much longer.

I carried the rear pole of a basket slung between Ishki and myself, and I struggled with the weight. Ishki made his end seem light, most likely to impress Mikala. My growl of jealousy was easily hidden within my panting gasps as we maneuvered over the rough ground up to the cavern entrance.

A raindrop struck my face. Then, suddenly....

...I was Ishki, a few years younger; alone, afraid, and crying over a fire that had killed both my parents and left me to the care of myself...

"Keep moving," Ishki hollered, prodding me back into myself. I took a step forward.

...And I was the old blacksmith, Timon, hammering a glob of red hot iron to glassy perfection...

...Then Nohn, the hunter who lived alone far from the village, as I gutted a fresh-killed black bear, blood spilling in great gouts as steam rose into the morning sky...

"What's wrong with you?" Mikala asked.

"N-Nothing." I shook off the raindrops, and the unsettling image.

...a young woman who looked just like the old midwife Eilssa, naked, howling at a gigantic summer moon...

The sensations continued, each impressing a moment of the lives of the people around me. Interspaced were flashes where I felt heavy, rooted, a dull thing with no thoughts other than an endless yearning for the sky. Once, I was a fox again, and I thought I'd explode into tears.

I endured these assaults. My outward attitude alternated between distraction, hysteria, and restlessness.

An old woman approached. She told me to go away. It was Eilssa, although much more ancient. I had not recognized her with her clothing on.

I stumbled through the trail back to the village in the direction of the black-smith's house, hoping to find my father. I needed reassurance. Icy rain had turned to snow, falling in fat little bundles that hit the ground like wet seagull turds. Some of the flakes struck me with no effect, frigid water melting harmlessly against my skin. Others crashed into me with the force of foreign memories, violating my mind, and imposing thoughts that were not my own.

With each strike, it became more bearable. I didn't stumble and fall when I learned the cruel bully everyone called Gol secretly wished he'd not been born a man. I simply pushed it away.

I suddenly felt I could push all those moments past the intensity of the present and into the back of my mind. Once behind me, they became only memories, and I could view them with a measure of detachment. Some were distressing, brutal, and perverse in that they revealed secrets about members of my village I didn't want to know. Others were interesting, and I learned several skills within the space of a single thought that I'd never hoped to master.

One snowflake touched my lips, a kiss of frost that brimmed with 'aiei. I didn't realize it at first, but one of my own memories had returned, borne on the western wind, ripe with magic.

...My father stood before me, that hopeful, happy expression on his face...

I reached out to him, but found myself rolling down a short ledge not far from the river.

When I finally arrived at the blacksmith's house, I found Moahb standing over my father's body. My father had died suddenly, rising from his chores and walking slowly towards the river before he collapsed. Moahb had come upon him as he lay sprawled against a boulder, cold, soaked through with the rain. It appeared as though he'd embraced the stone in his last moments.

Together, we brought him up to the master's house where I laid him out and covered him with blankets. Moahb wept copiously, but I did not cry. I'd known my father would die since the night of our hunting trip, and thinking back on his comments of that night, I believed he knew it as well. I don't think he wanted that knowledge to spoil our last moments together.

I held Moahb a while, feeling his small frame shake against me as he expressed his sorrow. The shock hadn't reached me yet. I thought it might never come. My quick acceptance might be a tangible benefit of the *'aiei*.

The whole of that last time with my father, our final and most meaningful bonding, flashed through me with the power and intensity of lightning. Then it faded in a backwash of diffuse energy against the snow, and I was no longer a boy.

Time hadn't passed. The mountains loomed behind my tired and aching body. I sat on a fallen log just as my father had at the beginning of that fateful day when he'd first shown me the power of magic, a dollop of frost resting on my tongue. Little Achlie crouched beside me. He hadn't stirred. His eyes still glittered like polished stones, like chunks of dark metal touched by my father's 'aiei.

An ice crystal struck my face. I saw my father again.

...He smiled at me, reaching out to stroke my cheek. He smiled at me from a memory found in a snowflake, from the 'aiei of winter...

I clenched my eyes shut, my hand tight on Achlie's shoulder, and held onto that image. I smiled back as I caught the twinkle in my father's dark eyes, so much like the forged plates of obsidian metal he worked so often. And, yes, I cried a little.

D. A. D'Amico is a crazy mix of clumsy mad scientist and failed evil wizard, leading to spectacular displays of truly unremarkable brilliance. Occasionally, the stars align, and a coherent storyline is born. He's had nearly eighty works published in the last decade in venues such as Daily Science Fiction, and Shock Totem, and his personal favorite, MYTHIC. He's a winner of L. Ron Hubbard's prestigious Writers of the Future award, volume XXVII, as well as the 2017 Write Well award. Collections of his work, links to anthologies and magazines he's be in can be found on Amazon at: https://www.amazon.com/D-A-DAmico. His website is: http://www.dadamico.com. Facebook: authordadamico, and on painfully rare occasions twitter: @dadamico.

The Dryad's Muse

By Tom Jolly

Dryads didn't have cell phones. Dr. Matt Hamilton looked at the clipboard for his scheduled patient, and not for the first time, wondered how some of the supernatural creatures that visited Redstone Clinic made appointments ahead of time.

"Thanks, Medjine."

The zombie receptionist nodded. "You are welcome, Dr. Hamilton. The patient is waiting for you in exam room two."

Hamilton never expected his career to involve curing monsters. It was pure chance that brought a werewolf to the clinic's door, and Hamilton's nature led him to sew up the bullet wound in its leg. It was never really a choice for him.

After that, all the supernatural creatures within the city seemed to have decided that he was the guy to go to; the one who would ask no questions and keep his mouth shut. So his patient list was a supernatural sampler of monsters and curiosities. Every day, a new flavor.

The dryad was his first patient of the day, though it was already 2PM; the clinic opened late and stayed open through the early evening hours to accommodate nocturnal patients. He wrote down the time on his clipboard. A dryad! He

knew a bit about them, but had never had one as a patient. Something new to deal with. He entered the exam room, not knowing what to expect.

The girl in the exam room was carrying a small potted red oak tree. She was strangely beautiful despite her green skin and hair made of strands of grass and tufts of leaves, moving as though a gentle breeze blew through the room. "Hello, Carielle" he said, "I'm Dr. Hamilton."

She saw him staring at the small tree and she held it up for him to see. "It's my home," she told him.

Hamilton wondered for a moment how she got here in the middle of a big city without arousing any comment or suspicion, but by now, he understood that everyone in the community had a few tricks up their sleeves to help blend in. He looked at his clipboard. "Carielle, I can't say I'm very familiar with dryads. Can you tell me a little about yourself?"

"I wanted to be an Earth Mother," she said, "but do you know how hard it is to find a nice earth elemental in the middle of a city?"

He shook his head. "No, I can't say that I do. So why not move out into the country?"

Carielle sighed. "You can't get a good espresso in the country."

Hamilton smiled. "Eternal love or good coffee. Always a tough choice."

She frowned. "Are you mocking me, mortal? Because I can..." she stopped and looked down at the little potted oak tree, and sighed. The branches twitched. "I can do very little."

Hamilton had to keep reminding himself that his patients weren't human, and some would just as soon tear his arm off as talk to him. "I'm sorry if I offended, Carielle," Hamilton said. "I was just making a little joke. Tell me what brings you to the clinic today."

She pulled her sleeve back and Hamilton winced. Her left hand was missing, sickly yellow veins trailing away from the stump up her arm. "My first home was over one hundred years old, on Willow Street. There was an old house there, and they tore it down to put in condos, and my tree was in the front yard. I knew they were coming soon to cut it down, but the oak had a sapling, and I had to move my belongings to this tiny home. I had to give away a lot of things."

Hamilton really wanted to ask her what things you could store in a three-foot tall oak sapling, or for that matter, a full-sized oak tree, but he resisted.

"When I transferred myself to the young oak, I found that it was sick. I took the sickness from it so it would thrive. It is part of being a dryad, keeping your home healthy. And the sickness should have died then, since they prefer the oak to the essence of our own bodies. But it came over to me, as though part of both worlds, the living and the magical."

Magical! Hamilton hated that word. He'd spent the last year trying to classify various creatures by their substances: what they were made of. If he could measure it and quantify it, he could start dealing with their illnesses in a more traditional fashion. In some ways, he felt like a doctor from the 1800's, trying to define bacterial diseases before they even knew that such things existed, excising the specter of "possession by spirits" that was so popular in those days. Not that that didn't actually happen on occasion, he'd discovered.

The dryad was part of a class of creatures who didn't require human belief, and could dematerialize when they needed to, or appear as solid when necessary. Their "cells," if you could call them that, could convert to a gaseous form that could merge with their host-tree. In most cases, when a group of creatures had similar abilities, such as the shapechanging were-creatures, they shared similar cell structures and were genetically close to one another on the evolutionary ladder. Though the dryad would be disgusted to know it, she was closely related to Bigfoot, sort of a giant, ugly, stinky dryad that could adopt an entire forest. He found it interesting that dryads could mate with earth elementals, putting them in the same cellular class. He itched to go write in his notebooks.

"Generally," Hamilton said, "diseases can't travel between species unless the species are very close. In your case, I suspect the disease you have is a mutation of a common oak disease. This is particularly bad for your community, because you can potentially act as a host for the disease and can spread it to other dryads if you have any social contact with them."

He took the stump of her arm in his hand and examined it. It was as light as balsa. The yellow veins tinged toward brown as they approached her stump. He sat back on his stool, picked his iPad up off the desk, and did a quick search on oak diseases. "The most common diseases in oaks are funguses. If we can identify the fungus, then we can find a systemic fungicide that should be able to treat it. The local nursery or arboretum can probably identify it if they have a sample."

"I have a sample you could give them," she said. She reached into a pouch made of woven grass and pulled out a shriveled brown object. He leaned over to stare at it. It was her missing hand.

"Hmm. I had something more like a leaf in mind. That might not go over well at a plant nursery." He picked up his iPad again. "Look, do you remember what the oak looked like when you took it over? Was it sick then?"

She nodded. "It looked so sad. Like a Charlie Brown Christmas tree."

"Charlie Brown? Your previous tree must have been near someone's TV set, I'm guessing." On his iPad, he brought up a website showing pictures of various oak afflictions, then flipped it around so she could see it. She gasped and put her hand over her mouth, pushing the screen away. "Oh! What a horrible machine!"

"I need you to identify the damage you saw on your little oak before you cured it. We might be able to figure out the fungicide needed to kill the infection."

She reluctantly took another look at the iPad. He scrolled down the page while she looked on in horror. Finally she said, "There! It looked like that!" Then she turned her head away. "The humans that created that are terrible people."

"This is here so others like me can find cures for these diseases. These are not bad people. They share these images to save trees."

She sniffed and wiped a tear away, mollified.

"It looked like oak wilt. Pretty common. The fungicide brand they mention here is called Alamo. If you can transfer the disease back to the oak, before you use the fungicide, it'll be safer for you. I don't know what it'll do to your existing body."

"That would be impossible. Would you give your child a disease to make yourself feel better?"

He drummed his fingers impatiently on the top of the iPad. "Okay, I see your point. But I'd like you to be here when we apply the stuff. If there's an adverse reaction, maybe we can control it."

She looked uncomfortable. "It's alright. But I have no place to stay. And there is no sun in here."

"There's rooftop access from a stairway in back. You can relax up there in the sun while we see if we can get some of the fungicide. I'll come up and get you, and we can run some tests." He stuck his head out the door of the exam room. "Agatha?" The Oracle was standing just outside the door, as if waiting for something. "Ah. Of course. Could you please guide Carielle to the rooftop stairwell? Once you're done with that, please pick up a bottle of this," he showed her a picture of the fungicide on the iPad. "Take some money out of petty cash for it. I'll be seeing my next patient while you're gone."

"He's in Room 1. Very moody fellow!" said Agatha.

Hamilton picked the clipboard up from Medjine's desk as he walked by the receptionist. He knocked and entered the exam room. The man inside was tall and thin, all angles and lines. A compass and a ruler stuck out of his pocket. He was pale and sickly, his clothing expensive but at the same time worn and shabby. "Hello, Doctor," he said. His voice was as rough as sandpaper.

"Hello Mr. Steel. I see you signed in as an architect's muse. You say you're feeling depressed? Weak and lethargic?"

"I try to whisper words of wisdom, design inspiration and aspiration, into the minds of youthful architects and builders! The beauty and simplicity of huge swathes of cement, the purity and geometric construction of perfect surfaces, smooth beyond comparison! But do they listen? No. They want confusion and chaos, nothing matches. Organic forms, they cry! They have ceased to listen to me." He hung his head. "I am dying."

Hamilton considered the creature. Muses fell into the category of very, very small gods. They existed because people believed they existed or wanted them to exist. They seemed to consist of a sort of matter that was related to thoughts just as light was associated with matter. But this implied that thoughts actually had some sort of reality like photons, and could be converted into the thought-matter that gods and spirits were made of. Like the association between light and matter, he assumed it took quite a lot of thought to coalesce into an entity like this. But there was no E=mc2 in what everyone else called the supernatural realm. At least, not yet.

"You were larger before this, I take it?"

"Oh, huge! Very popular in Russia. My head could barely fit through a doorway, so large was I. But even there the interest has faded."

Hamilton scratched his head. "I don't understand. If you are *the* muse for architectural design, and architects are ignoring you, how is it that they have any great ideas?"

Steel shrugged. "Some dullards use old ideas and copy them, or perhaps something completely unrelated to architecture inspires them. Sometimes evil muses in other arenas of creativity cross over the line, afflicting the minds of willing slaves with their witless ideas! Like the muse to birds, teaching architects how to make beautiful nests in China! See how that turned out?"

"So your sickness appears to be something that a doctor like me can't cure. I can't change the thoughts that will keep you from wasting away. I can't tell you how to do your job, but I'm guessing that a muse has to follow the basic leads of his...subjects...and expand on the creative directions they already wish to pursue. For example, a writer's muse wouldn't try to influence a fantasy writer to write a medical thriller, would she?" Hamilton asked.

"But the very fundamental nature of architecture is mathematics," the muse replied. "The purity of a flat plane, a perfect cube, the exactly executed circle, these are the firmaments upon which I am built! How can I defy my very nature as a muse of mathematics to...to...educate these simpletons!"

Hamilton chuckled.

"What do you find so amusing, doctor?"

"You just called yourself a 'muse of mathematics'. Perhaps you aren't dying. Maybe you're just changing professions."

His eyes darted around the office, anxiously, his hands trembling. "But I *like* buildings! Math and buildings belong together! They will fall down if I am not there to guide the architect's befuddled thoughts."

"So I suppose it'd be important to find out what other influences are affecting their creative processes and add your little spark of brilliance."

"Not just a 'little spark', but yes, perhaps."

Hamilton sat down on the stool and thought for a moment. "Recently," he said, "a lot of new architects have been moving toward greener designs. Things that incorporate gardens, trees, and lots of plants. Terraced areas, hanging gardens, green walls, that sort of thing."

"But plants are so chaotic! Messy and unaligned."

Hamilton's thoughts drifted back to the dryad. Plants. Chaotic plants. But they weren't, really. "Are you familiar with fractals at all?"

"Yes. No. Not so much."

"It turns out that plant growth obeys certain mathematical rules. There's a bit of chaos in there; I suppose humans are naturally attracted to that at some level. But basically, plants obey the same fundamental mathematics that your buildings contain."

"I...think I see."

Hamilton tapped slowly on the clipboard, thinking. Could the muse use a muse? "I'd like you to meet someone. She might be able to help you expand your creative horizons."

"They are already as vast as the seas," Steel said. He looked down at the floor, and sighed. "But I will try almost anything at this point."

The two of them stepped out onto the roof. The area around the clinic was hilly, and the tops of dozens of other buildings were visible nearby, trees towering over many of them. In one corner of the roof, gathering the Sun's rays, was a small potted oak tree. As they watched, a misty cloud coalesced around the small oak tree and materialized into a solid form.

"Hello, Carielle," said Hamilton.

"Hello, Doctor. Have you retrieved the medicine so soon?"

"No, not yet." He paused and turned to Steel. "I'd like you to meet Steel. He's a muse of architecture."

Her face turned red. "A minion of death! Covering life with barren cement abortions!"

Steel just stared at her. "She's very pretty."

Hamilton almost laughed, but refrained. "The muse needs your help. He needs to learn how to adapt his musings to include plants."

She tilted her chin up in the air and

turned her side to them, managing to look insulted and smug all at the same time. "Why would I ever help such an atrocious beast as this thing?"

Steel saw the stump of her hand. "You're hurt!" He stepped toward her.

"Stop!" she cried, holding out the other hand.

His chest thumped into her extended hand. He looked down at it and backed away, a wan look on his face. "It has been thus since the Hanging Gardens," he said, head hanging down.

Hamilton was stunned into silence for a moment, remembering that muses were essentially immortal. "...of Babylon?" he asked.

A look of consternation crossed the muse's face. "Yes, I think it was called that. The terraced gardens. The vines overgrew the sides, hanging down from terrace to terrace. The twisted trunks of jasmine and grape vines climbed the walls like trunks of stone. It could have lasted forever." He put his hand on his forehead, tears welling up in his eyes. "But a visiting prince and his mistress came to the gardens, and she ate of the fruits and nuts hanging from the trees and bushes and vines. What she was allergic to, no one knows, but she died that very night. The gardens were burned to the ground the next day, and the architect, my friend and student, was tied hand and foot and given to the prince's dogs to eat. I have never suggested such a design to my students since then."

"The Hanging Gardens? You were the muse for *The Gardens*?" Carielle shouted.

"I was. I vowed never again to cause the death of a student."

Hamilton watched Carielle shake. He couldn't tell if it was from rage or something else entirely. He'd never seen such a confusion of expressions on a face before, flickering across her countenance like a lightning storm. Was she going to kill him or hug him?

"I will help you!" she finally screamed at him. "We will see gardens that will make humans weep with joy when they set their eyes upon them! The trunks of mighty oaks will be the pillars of towering temples of life!"

Steel peered at her askance and started to say, "There would be certain structural considerations using trees..." but she ran to him and clutched him in a powerful embrace, weeping in joy.

He patted her arm and looked dubiously at Hamilton. Then the muse smiled and nodded. And grew a little taller.

Of course, the muse wasn't exactly a substitute for an earth elemental. Hamilton wondered how an ephemeral creature made of thought-particles was going to relate to a gaseous phase-changing creature like Carielle, but had a feeling it would work out. Somehow.

He also thought about mentioning the fact that humans understood a lot more about allergies and poisons than they used to, and were much less inclined to feed peons to the dogs these days. But now was not the time.

He retreated to the stairs. They could take care of themselves.

Carielle visited Hamilton a year later to thank him for his help. Her hand had grown back by then, and she was literally glowing with verdant health.

"The giant structure downtown, that's your doing?"

"That is Steel's doing. The thousands of trees and vines on each terraced level are mine." She smiled an Earth Mother's smile. "The glass terrarium capping the top was a combined effort."

"It looks like someone imported a Mayan pyramid into the middle of Los Angeles."

Carielle nodded, long grass and leaves rippling atop her head like wind in a forest. "A thousand homes and offices, and four thousand trees. I am the Earth Mother of that urban forest. It has set an example. Other dryads in the city have begun...securing...human architects."

"You mean seducing?"

She shrugged. "The architects involved have not been unhappy, I think."

Hamilton laughed and shook his head. She smiled shyly at him, and he couldn't decide whether to pity or envy the architects.

TOM JOLLY is a retired astronautical/electrical engineer who now spends his time writing SF and fantasy. His stories have appeared in Analog SF, Daily SF, Compelling SF, MYTHIC, and a number of anthologies. His latest book, "An Unusual Practice," about a doctor whose patients tend toward the supernatural, is currently available on Amazon. To find more of his stories, visit www.silcom.com/~tomjolly/tomjolly2.htm.

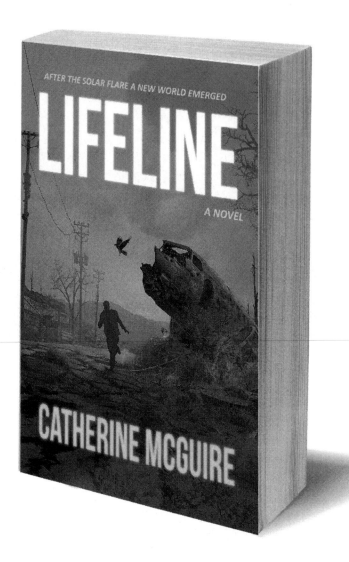

AFTER THE SOLAR FLARE A NEW WORLD EMERGED

LIFELINE

A NOVEL

CATHERINE MCGUIRE

Fifty years after a massive solar flare ravages modern industrial civilization, a young man named Martin Barrister has a difficult job. He must attempt to e-establish communication links with the rest of the country. Yet, things aren't what they seem. The world outside New York City is very different and he may be caught up in a web of dangerous dealing and potential warfare.

Available in paperback and electronic editions.

A Dragon Bigger Than My Stories

By Jonathon Mast

Every dragon's an introvert. Why else would they hide in caves? They hate small talk as much as I do.

But that's why I love my dragon so much.

I'm up on the roof, looking over gray Londinium. Smokestacks raise their middle fingers toward the sky, belching out their rotten perfumes. The Gears of the city grind out their music over the constant babble of the crowds on the streets below. Tiny pinpricks of snow try to blot out the sound as they pelt my face. My fingers will freeze if I stay out here too much longer. The wind is scattering my long hair and turning my snot to ice. I'm probably not the prettiest girl in the city right now. Or ever.

But I don't care. I have a dragon.

She told me her name once, but I can't speak her language. Not really. I tried saying it out loud, but making my mouth say her name was like making a Gear out of snow. It just didn't work. So she's just my dragon, and I'm just her human.

There she is. She darts through the pillars of smoke, snatching up all the gulls she can.

I laugh.

After she gobbles up another half-dozen birds she arches into the marble sky and then down toward me. Her almost-white beak seems to curve into a smile as she makes eye contact with me. Her magnificent pale-blue wings flutter as she sets down on the roof, her four taloned feet touching down on the rough slate. Her shoulder comes up just short of my shoulder, and even with all the muscle on her body, she seems as light as I am.

She comes and nuzzles into me. *Are you hungry?* she whispers into my mind. She doesn't really use words, but I understand most of what she whispers fine. At least that bit about hunger.

No, I lie.

There's a rumble deep in her throat. *You need food.*

I get enough. I glance back at the door that leads to the stairs, back down into the heat and the cram of bodies. *I should get back.*

I will take you to my home, she whispers. *When I am large enough.*

I smile and hug her head, patting her curved beak and looking into her golden eyes. *I can't wait.*

She sends me a picture. A cave. No Gears. No people. No smoke. Plenty of

43

food. And there we are, me and her. I give her everything she needs, and she gives me everything I need.

Feed me, she pleads.

You just ate!

Feed me. Her golden eyes bore into mine.

And I know what she means. She needs more than the meat of pigeons. And so I glance again at the door.

Maybe we can take a little time.

I speak out loud, stroking her pale-blue scales, feeling their warmth and their surprising softness. "Once upon a time a girl named Ash Anna was abandoned at an orphanage. But she had been left by mistake, for her parents were still alive and ruled in a faraway land. She told the orphanage mistress over and over again, but no one believed her. Or maybe they did. Because every child in the orphanage was a princess." And I tell my dragon the whole story, from the grinding poverty and the hard worl and how all the princesses learn how to make something of themselves, and how they eventually banded together to free the thirty princes captured by the troll.

And they live happily ever after.

I always tell her stories of heroes. Always. Because I wish I had a hero to rescue me. Well, I used to. Now I have my dragon, and that's even better.

My dragon rumbles an almost-purr. *I am full.* She coils up on the roof, her long tail wrapping around her. I almost think I can see her grow. Good.

The stories feed her. And I am the best storyteller of all the grinding girls.

The dorms are hot, and the humidity clings to me. Three girls already pack into my bed. Ten opens one eye as I try to shove her over. "You wasn't at supper."

"I'm not hungry," I answer.

"Who's he?" She's still only got the one eye open.

"He?"

"You're gonna end up pregnant, you keep going out like that. You know the boys don't marry us. Don't matter what he says." Ten spits out the last words.

"I'm not seeing a boy." The thought disgusts me. I know some girls hope they can get out by finding some man, but life doesn't really work that way. Besides, any boy who would look at me that way would probably be mad.

"You're seeing a girl? That'll get you ground out so fast!" Ten leers at me.

I hit her.

She giggles, waking the other two.

Of course the story is around the dorm twice before I can fall asleep, and by then everyone's talking about how I sell girls to upper-class ladies and if anyone wants to get out of the dorms, come see me.

I can't wait for my dragon to take me away.

The coal pours down the chute. "C'mon, girls!" cries Patty Rinkin, one of the only ones of us that merit a last name. She's angry. She's always angry when she's hungry, and like the rest of us, she's always hungry.

We all groan. It's only the third load today, but the cold is making us stiff. It's always cold here. Gotta keep the coal from lighting. We stuff what we can into our bags and trudge back to our tables over by the Gears to grind down the larger chunks into usable size.

I shout out over the constant deep rumble, "So Constance, she changes her mind. She lays down the sword. The sunset reflects off it. The Goblin King raises an eyebrow and his blade to strike."

The girls around me gasp. The stories pass the time. And it's good to know someone gets a happy ending, even if it's just made up. Even if I just made it up now. I grab another chunk of coal twice the size of my head and put it against the spinning gears. Black dust fills the air. I cough before continuing.

"Constance smiles. 'I'll trade you,' she says. The Goblin King chokes back a cry of rage. 'No! You know a goblin can never resist a trade!' And the girl, she just smiles at him. She finally figured it out. You can't defeat a goblin with steel, but you can with your wit."

The coal in my hand sparks. I cut off the story as I pull back. No fires here. That would be bad. Senny was in one of the fires. Now all she does is sweep the stairs over and over again.

And I glance down at the coal, and then again.

And I swear.

A stone the color of the sky and the size of my thumbnail sits in the middle of the coal chunk.

Another dragon egg.

I manage to smuggle it back to the dorms by tucking it up in my mouth. Tastes about as good as you'd expect.

Ten grabs me before I can get up to the roof. "'Ey! You goin' walkin' with the boy again?" She winks.

"I'm visiting the House of Lords!" I mumble around the egg and trot off to take a seat in the crappery instead. It stinks, but hey, at least I'm alone here. I spit out the egg and spit some more to get the lurking taste of coal out of my gob. Nasty stuff.

It's the same blue that my dragon's egg was. The same smooth texture. The same size.

How many eggs do dragons lay? Well, considering that my dragon was the first dragon I'd ever even heard of outside a story, maybe no one knows.

Someone knocks on the door. "Be done in a gear's turn!" I answer and start putting myself back together, slipping the egg back into my mouth.

Patty Rinkin's waiting for me, her arms crossed. "Girls tell me you've been slipping out."

I roll my eyes.

"Girls tell me you've been seeing someone."

I roll my eyes again. I don't want to talk; the egg's in my mouth and would make me sound funny. Ten might not notice, but Patty would. Or she'd think I was drunk. That would make her even more angry.

"Girls tell me you ain't been visited by Bloody Jane for a bit."

I raise my eyebrow. Like any of them would know if I was pregnant! Or that anyone would ever want to have a baby with me. Or do what it takes to have a baby.

And that's when I feel the egg heat up in my mouth.

Oh no. Patty's telling stories. And the

dragon in my gob's feeding on them. It was probably eating all the stories I told in the grindery today, and it only needs a little more. Yep. There's a seam forming in the stone as I run my tongue over it.

"Girls tell me lots of things, Manda. And I noticed, too, that you're not eatin' much. Maybe because you've got the morning heaves. Maybe you're in a family way with no family. And you know the mistress don't abide by us doin' any such hanky-panky, does she?"

I spit out a dragon.

Patty screams.

I slap her.

She shuts her mouth. She looks down at the wrinkled blue form I caught in my hands. It's tiny; barely a tadpole, really. I keep spitting. The stony remains of the egg fly from my mouth. I peer back into my hand. The thing's wings are wrapped tight around its body so it looks like a long snake. Its eyes aren't open.

Patty wrinkles her nose. "That ain't the morning heaves."

I laugh.

Her eyes snap up at me. "You get this from some gearboy?"

The little dragon in my hand shifts weakly. It needs food. I don't really have a choice.

I answer, "Let's go up to the roof. Let me tell you a story."

My dragon is displeased that someone else is on her roof. She circles the distant pillars of smoke, refusing to come any nearer.

I understand.

Patty is pacing, stomping back and forth on the roof. Someone's going to hear the noise and come up. And then more people will be here. Already there's too many people.

Patty points up at my dragon. "So she's been flying around up there for how long?"

"About a month. Probably since the girls started noticing I was gone." I refuse to look at Patty. Instead I hold the little dragon. It drank in the story. Now it roams the contours of my palm, sniffing between my fingers and looking up at me. I can hear it whispering, but it doesn't have anything resembling language yet. It's more like the grinding of a very small gear.

"How come no one noticed him?"

"Her. And how often do you look up?"

"Hm." She frowns, stops pacing, crosses her arms, starts pacing again.

I don't want her up here. The back of my head aches. This is my space. My place for me and my dragon. Today it's not snowing, and there's a few shafts of sunlight coming down through the clouds. The Gears are loud and tugging their way into my head. At least the crowds of the street seem quieter.

"How do you know it's a her?"

I shrug. "I just know."

"What are you doing with her?"

I look up at my dragon. She's still circling over there, through the smoke, her wide, wide wings like a stab of sky that's come down below the clouds. "I'm not doing anything with her. She's her own dragon." Why should I tell Patty my plans?

She frowns. "So this one's mine then?" She gestures to the little guy now nestled in my palm and sleeping.

I pull back my hand, jarring the little one awake. "No! You can't own a dragon!"

"I thought you said that one was your dragon!"

I press my lips together. My space. My dragons. And Patty's invading all of it, clanging like a gear out of place and the wrong size besides. Gumming up all my thinking, all my hopes.

How can I have a happy ending if there's another person there?

Patty and I sort of end it by just walking away. She goes back for supper. I stay on the roof. My dragon comes to me. She isn't too happy to see the little one in my hand but greets me as always. *Are you hungry?*

No, I lie.

You need food.

You need stories. And with that I begin. "Once upon a time there was a girl so ugly that no man would ever look at her. But she had a secret. Because no one would look at her, she could do whatever she wanted. So she left the city one day and found a forest."

My dragon snorts. *My story!*

I stop. *What?*

He's eating it!

I look down in my palm. The little dragon is awake, its long tail lashing, looking up at me hungrily and clacking its tiny beak.

You can't share?

Dragons don't share food, she answers, *lifting her head with a snort. And you are my human. Dragons don't share humans.*

What am I supposed to do?

Get that other one. The dirty one. She's *good enough for that.* She stalks off to the other side of the roof.

I set the new dragon down on the slate. It paws around in a circle a few times and then looks up at me. "Wait here," I tell it, and turn back to the door. I take a deep breath. I can send Patty and the dragon down to the yard, but so many of the girls go back there, if nothing else than for the crappery. They'd be found out so fast. The only place for them is here.

The only place is here.

I look down at the dragon again. All right. Fine. But only because of the dragon.

Patty stumbles through a bunch of stories. It's clear she has no clue what she's doing. She keeps going backwards and retelling things because she gets it wrong or forgets something or adds in random details. The stories are twisted, stunted, angry little things. Not the kinds of stories I like. It's like she never listened to me when I told my stories at the grindery.

Ouch. That one hurts. All I am is my stories. I got nothing else. I don't have looks or strength or money or friends or even a chest, really, but I can tell stories. That should be enough.

But if someone doesn't listen to my stories, I'm nothing.

My dragon can tell I'm anxious, though, and she nuzzles into me. My stories are enough for her. And at the rate she's growing, maybe just a few more days and she can fly me away to wherever this cave is that she remembers from before she was an egg.

47

How can you remember something from before you were an egg? I ask.

She blinks. *Can't you?*

The Gears seem louder at the grindery today. Maybe my ears are already adjusting to the forest I'm looking forward to. I call out over the noise, "And Tristam stood before the Aeropterex. He drew his Gearblade, the metal lengthening as the machinery locked into place. 'Return Dulcet to me!' he cried."

Ten screams next to me. I jump to my feet, ready to pull her back from the Gears. Did they snag one of her fingers? An entire hand?

But all she does is hold up a piece of coal.

No. Another dragon's egg.

She peers at it, and the other girls gather around. "It's so pretty!" one says. Patty hops down from her coal chute. "Get back to work! Back to work!" she hollers until she sees what Ten holds. Her eyes dart to me.

I shrug.

But it is no longer just a stone in her hand. Its nature can't be hidden. It ate too much of my story. It shakes.

She drops it to her table.

Around us, the Gears continue to turn.

The blue stone cracks open and a tiny dragon emerges. It stumbles around the work station, trying to find its balance.

Half the girls scream and back away. The other half step closer and exclaim about how cute it is.

I imagine what my dragon would say. *Not cute. Regal.*

I see Patty sigh. She raises her eyebrows at me.

Oh, no. She wants me to explain. She wants me to tell them. I don't want to. I can tell stories. But then they'll pelt me with questions and they'll pry into my space and maybe that'll mean more people on the roof and my dragon won't come to me while they're there and I need my dragon

Stop.

You can do this, Manda. Just tell them the story and feed the baby dragon.

Fine.

And so I say, "Girls, this isn't the first dragon that's come from the coal. Let me tell you how I found my dragon."

She's really not happy. Neither am I. Patty on the roof was a grinding Gear. Now a whole cacophonous Machine sounds in the back of my head, at my temples, through all of me.

All the girls are on the roof.

Their prattle drowns out the Gears, the crowds below, everything. I can't hear anything else.

My dragon circles the rising smoke again. And all the girls ask their questions. They're mostly good questions. I still want them gone. I answer what I can.

Yesterday's dragon snuggles up against Patty. He's grown to be about the size of a cat, though a very awkward cat. Apparently Patty's stories didn't feed her as well as my stories nourish my dragon. I take no small pride in that. Maybe you are the stories you hear.

The new dragon rests in Ten's palm. Since she found the egg, I guess it's fair.

And really, I only need one dragon, as she reminded me yesterday. Ten's a better storyteller than Patty, too, but still not as good as me. She's telling stories about tricksters. Those are good. Not as good as hero stories, though.

The rest of the girls try sitting on the roof, but it's pretty cold up here, and the slate freezes them. They stand around for a while. When it's clear my dragon isn't coming, most go back into the dorm. Ten takes her dragon with. Before they go, though, I look at all of them. "You can't tell anyone. We don't know what they'd do."

Really, I just want to make sure they stay quiet until my dragon can take me away. I don't care what happens after that.

I don't.

The girls all nod solemnly. They're used to keeping secrets. Not from each other, but everyone knows about the dragons now.

Just Patty stays on the roof, trying to feed her dragon stories. After a while she says to me, "It's nice up here. All alone."

I grunt.

"I get why you come up here now."

I grunt again.

Finally, after a few more stories, Patty leaves, and her dragon curls up to sleep. Finally my dragon lands, and it's just me and her. *Are you hungry?* she asks.

No, I lie. *Are you hungry?*

She comes to me. My head only reaches her shoulder now. She grows so fast. I wrap my arms around her neck, and she rumbles her approval. We hold each other for a while.

I love my dragon because she will never tell anyone when I cry.

The next day three more girls find dragon's eggs. Jealousy abounds. I am glad my dragon is mine and no one can take her away from me. I am told the dorm is alive with stories that night. The girls are trying to remember the stories I always make up in the grindery. Let them reuse those old things.

I tell my dragon stories no one else has ever known. Just her and me.

And Patty and her dragon, who have taken to the roof.

My dragon snorts at Patty.

Patty sticks her tongue out. "It's too loud down there now. And my dragon probably shouldn't go down." Her dragon is a slightly darker blue, and he looks thinner than mine did at that age. But he's gotten up to be about mid-thigh height, and Patti hugs him. "What are we going to do with six dragons when they're all as big as yours?" she asks me.

I don't answer. What should I care?

We should find a quiet place, a strange voice whispers at me. I jump.

Patty laughs. "I don't know what I'd do in a place without the Gears. Next you'll be saying we should find a place without smoke."

I whisper to my dragon, *I can hear other dragons?*

Why not? she answers. *You can hear many humans. Why not many dragons?*

I don't want to hear any other dragons. Just you.

She rumbles her purr again. *I don't want any other humans.*

I sleep curled up with my dragon. She's big enough to protect me from the wind, mostly. Patty tries curling up with hers, but he's just not big enough to give her enough warmth. She's not feeding him well. The next morning I watch dawn over Londinium. Cold white light shoots through the city from the east, pouring through the thick clouds, making the shadows of the smokestacks even deeper. The Gears pound on, as they ever do, and in the streets people go about their clockwork dance. But above I snuggle into my dragon.

Patty rubs her eyes. "It's actually kinda pretty, ain't it?"

I offer half a smile. "It's only pretty when there ain't people around."

"You ever think about taking your dragon and flying away?"

I look at her. I look at her dragon. I lie.

No one's paying attention in the grindery today. They all stayed up late telling stories. I really don't want to deal with the screaming that comes from accidents here, though. There's plenty of bloodstains on the Gears already. Patty knows it. She's yelling louder than normal for everyone to pay attention.

The girls that are awake are watching their coal closely. They want their own dragons. Thankfully no one tried smuggling their dragons in this morning. Some of them might have been dumb enough to try, but Patty nixed that right away. Maybe she is good for something.

"Why do you think we keep finding eggs?" Ten asks next to me as she carefully grinds down some more coal.

"I was talking with my dragon about that."

"Wait – they talk?" she exclaims.

"Yeah. Kind of. Yours probably will today or tomorrow if you're feeding it well enough. Anyway, we think their mom laid all the eggs in the coal deposit. And the miners just took all the coal out, didn't notice the eggs, and sent them here for processing."

"Oh." Ten grinds away. "Do they remember their mom?"

"I get images of a dragon every once in a while. I guess they remember things from before they were eggs. I don't get it."

Ten giggles a little. "I'm sorry I thought you were sneaking off with a boy. This is so much cooler."

I look down. Yeah. It is cooler, isn't it?

Only two more dragon eggs found that day.

Only.

What has my life become?

Thankfully I don't have to teach anyone anything anymore. Not so thankfully, soon the dragons will be too big to keep in the dorm. And I'm like my dragon. I don't like sharing. This might be my last night alone with her.

Well, with her and Patty and her dragon.

My dragon's shoulder is a good foot above my head now. I hope the roof is strong enough to hold all of us. Then again, she's still lighter than I'd ever think, almost like a bird. Maybe that's how she flies so well, gliding through the air.

As I come to the roof, she lands as far from Patty as possible. *Are you hungry?*

No, I lie.

Soon, she answers. *Tomorrow. Feed me well tonight, and tomorrow we will be gone.*

I don't even care that Patty sees me crying.

In the morning the dawn comes over Londinium. The cold, white light pours over everything. Today some gentle snow settles over the city. The Gears seem quieter.

And my dragon seems to smile at me. *Are you hungry?*

My grin must be so wide. I hug her face as hard as I can. *Let's go. Let's go now before Patty wakes up.*

My dragon kneels before me, and I scramble on to her back. Her pale blue scales are so soft and so warm. I hug her thick neck. I am ready to go.

She stands, and I almost fall off.

I have never been ridden before.

I've never ridden anything! I almost laugh.

Hold on. She spreads her wings, so large now, wider than the dorm, wider than I think she would ever need to be able to soar through the sky. She jumps.

And we are flying.

We're flying!

The dawn reaches out to grab at us, to suck us in. My dragon flaps her wings, and we rise to the heavens. The smokestacks couldn't reach us now. I let my laugh out. My joy fills the sky. No one can reach us! No one can talk to us! My dragon and I, we are alone at last, and even the sound of the Gears seems so far away. The city is small below us, all snow and shadows, its people vanished in the distance. I couldn't pick out the dorm if I tried.

Then a shadow blots out the sun. Darkness and cold claim me.

I thought my dragon was large. But this dragon dwarfs the smokestacks. Larger than the Gears that power the city. Larger than my wildest story. She flies on wings that crack the sky. When she lands, the boom of it overpowers the Gears. But even in her size, I can see: She is starving. She looks like Patty's dragon writ large. She has had no story for a very, very long time. And the stories she grew on made her very, very angry.

I have never heard silence before this. The Gears have stopped. The city has stopped.

Londinium cannot face this dragon.

Her scales are the blue of midnight. Her beak is stained red. Her golden eyes take in everything. And her whisper is quieter than anything I have ever heard, but I cannot turn away from it. *I have scented them from my nest to here. Now. Give me my children.*

The silence ends. The screams begin. This huge dragon waits a moment, a moment more, and then takes a step. A smokestack falls. A fire breaks out.

Fly! I tell my dragon. And she turns and flies away. Her wings beat faster than I have ever seen her move. The wind tears at my face.

This is my dragon. This other dragon may have laid her, but I raised her. She is mine.

And you are mine, my dragon answers. I hear her fear. She does not want to be claimed.

I hear another smokestack fall. I am sure the city will not recover. Who could survive without the Gears?

I could.

Of course I could. I was planning to survive without them.

All those people, though. How many people will the mother crush? And if my dragon is with me, far away, will she ever stop destroying the city? How many will die? How many packed in together, sharing sweaty beds in the humidity, laughing too loud with each other, serving the Gears together?

No. It's not my problem. All I need is my dragon. She can hunt for me. And I can tell her stories. I can tell her all the stories of all the heroes.

Of all the heroes who stood up to the monsters.

Heroes who helped people, even when the people didn't care.

Heroes who faced impossible odds and had their happily ever afters.

I feel my hands bunch up into fists. I can fly away. All I ever wanted in blue scales. All she ever wanted, in the stories I tell.

I don't want to do this.

But you are the stories you tell.

I know what would stop her.

She's angry because she's hungry and she wants her children. I can solve both.

Turn around, I whisper.

Why?

We can save the city.

Why?

I can't answer for a moment. *She needs a story.*

My dragon glides for a moment. She banks, and we race back to Londinium. Back to smoke. Back to people and chaos and everything I hate. Back to face the monster.

Put me down—there. On that roof. Then go get the other dragons.

She lands, her claws scraping against the slate roof. I slide off her back, giving her a brief hug. *Come back for me.*

You are my human. And with that, she flies away.

My dragon's mother looms over me. She doesn't see me. How could she? I feel the heat come off of her. It's not a comfortable heat like my dragon. It burns like the Gears on a summer's day. She lifts one claw larger than the dorms. It crashes down on the building next to me. Dust shoots into the air. I hear screaming. Her next step will destroy the roof I stand on.

Are my words enough to feed a creature this big? I'm not good enough. I've never been good enough.

I think of my dragon. I'm good enough for her.

I shout. The first word hurts so much to scream so loud, but she must hear me. She must. "Once upon a time there was a girl who wanted to be alone, but she lived with a home full of people. She longed to find solitude, but all she found were elbows in her ear while she slept and knees in her porridge when she ate."

The claw before me doesn't move. I hear her dark scales flex as she turns her long neck toward me. Eyes taller than me narrow.

I don't have time for relief. I don't have time for fear. I have to feed her.

"Her mother needed her, though. So every day she swept the house and made the bread and tucked her brothers and sisters into bed. Every day she did what she must."

She did what she must.

Oh, my throat hurts so much. The words don't weave themselves the way they usually do; I can tell I'm thinking too hard. I'm trying to make the story cleverer by half, and I don't have that in me. Not when I face a dragon bigger than my stories.

But I tell her. I tell her what it is to be a hero. To know what you want, to set it aside, to do what must be done to rescue others. Even if it means giving up everything you always wanted. It seems like I tell my story for hours until I reach the conclusion. "And so she stayed in the home, and every day she visited the grave of her mother. And there she was alone. But she always went back to the little house to take care of her brothers and sisters, until the day she died."

And then my dragon arrives. She bears several small dragons the size of cats and dogs on her back, trying to teach them to fly and fly quickly. Patty's dragon follows on shaking wings. They all land next to me.

The mother breathes in, scenting them. *My children. Are you hungry?*

My dragon looks at me before answering, *We were well fed.*

My belly has been sated in small measure. The story nourishes me. Whose human is this?

Mine.

The huge dragon nods. *Dragons do not share humans.*

And my dragon trembles. *We do not.*

She raises herself tall in the sky above us. *I am hungry.*

And suddenly I realize I have not just delayed my dream of running away for a little bit. I turn to my dragon. "No!" I shout. I don't even care that I'm not whispering. I know she can understand. "I belong to you!"

She nuzzles me. *You have told me about heroes.* She pauses. I didn't know dragons could cry. *I am the stories you've told me.*

"Will she take me away?"

Yes.

"I don't want to leave you."

We may flee. But everyone here will die. Her anger will be fierce. She is angry when she is hungry.

"Come with."

She needed to make sure we were fed. Her job as mother is done. But dragons live alone. I cannot come with.

"Find me."

And now I cry, too. We hold each other.

I am hungry, the powerful, powerful whisper tells us.

"Fine then." I step away from my dragon. I sniff. *Are you hungry?* I ask her.

No, she lies.

And the mother picks me up in a claw that could house all the girls. She places me on her broad, broad back. Feed me as I fly, she commands. And she spreads her wings, wings wider than I can see, and she lifts off from the ground. Nothing this large should be able to fly, and yet she does.

And I feed her. I tell her all my stories.

I am old now. Probably close to death. The dragon who took me is not. Dragons are as old and as young as the stories they devour.

I have wanted for nothing. Silk clothing and rich food. I have been as alone

53

as I could ever wish.

But I long for my dragon. But dragons do not share food. Dragons do not share their humans.

I have heard that Patty and her dragon now protect Londinium. The girls have grown their clutch of dragons and are well taken care of. The Gears have stopped turning, and people grow things now. I cannot imagine such a place. I asked the dragon who owns me to take me there, but she refused.

But Londinium would have been destroyed had I not fed this dragon. And the girls would have died for nothing. I would be happy yes, but at what cost?

And my dragon.

My dragon is out there. I hope she is happy. I hope she has found someone to feed her.

No, I did not find my happily ever after. But I am a hero. They will tell my story until after Londinium has sunk to memories.

Jonathon Mast lives in Kentucky with his wife and an insanity of children. (A group of children is called an insanity. Trust me.) You can find him at https://wantedonenewearth.wordpress.com/

Still

By Erica Ruppert

I should have died a hundred years ago, a thousand. More years ago even than that, I'm sure, with the stars spinning by on their wheel so many times I've lost count. The world awakened me when it found I'd left it again, another form shed. And then it birthed me anew, unwilling.

My father led our tribe for many years, and his father before him, and his father before him as tradition demanded. But my father had no sons that lived, and so it came to be that I led our tribe when he died. There was some complaint at the change in tradition, but I was well-enough supported and well-enough liked that the grumbling soon quieted. Life went on much as it ever had, except a woman led. It was not as large a change as it seemed at first. But a change does not need to be large to be a threat.

I did not ask for anything different, nothing more or less that we had always done. We still built our houses on the slope above the river. We still tended our gardens and hunted the sheep, and deer, and antelope. We still gathered stores against the long barren winter. We still believed our priests could speak with the gods for us, to plead our case and offer our gratitude.

I put out of my mind that the priests still had their sons to think of.

In my fourth year as leader, our fortunes turned. Spring began, and as suddenly stopped. A great storm blew through and turned the world cold again. Buds froze on the branches. Animals died in their nests.

We struggled. The cold spring lasted, dissolving into a chill, wet summer. Not even the oldest of us could remember such cold lasting as it did. We starved, slowly. I led hunts. I foraged with my people. I ate less than my due, that they would have a little more.

We starved, but we did not die. We survived the barren summer, the lean fall, the damp and muddy winter that followed.

It was not enough.

When the next spring came, the gods of the sky told the priests that a woman could no longer lead the tribe. I did not believe them. But my people did. They looked at me now as if in wonder of how I could have led them at all. They chose to forget that I had suffered with them.

55

They let the priests confine me to my house while prayers were said and preparations made. I would be a sacrifice, to show the gods they would be worthy of mercy in the year to come.

For a full day and night they prayed, and sang, danced and burned herbs outside my door. To escape the drone of their voices I slept. Alone in my house, I dreamed of a voice like the whine of a wolf, like the yip of a fox. It rose and fell and told me that soon no women would lead us, and then no one at all. We would be set aside like old memories.

On the second morning they allowed my eldest sister, Ayedene, to enter and bid me goodbye. We had grown apart in our adulthood, but she claimed the right of kinship in order to see me. The priests would not deny that, not with our people watching and hoping for the gods to be kind.

As we knelt together on the rug, Ayedene pulled a tiny, leaf-wrapped packet from her belt. She unwrapped it and handed me the flat oval stone it contained.

"You tried, Damina," Ayedene said. "I cannot stop this, but I will do what I can to steer it. I will miss you."

I looked at the stone. It was a fleck of pink quartz the size of a fingernail, its luster dulled by the delicate figures painted on it.

"It is a charm, to help in what will come. Keep it under your tongue until you must swallow it."

She squeezed my hands between hers. I pressed my forehead to hers. We did not cry. I put the stone in my mouth and nodded. She smiled at me without joy, and left me to my end. Or so I believed.

My people buried me high above the village. They covered my mouth with cloth to still my screams, and bound my arms and legs with leather cords to still my thrashing. They dug my hole deep, to still me. They covered me with a flat-faced boulder and scratched my image into it. They gave me huge, round eyes to watch over them with, and a mouth full of sharp teeth to defend them with.

I screamed for a long time, until the dirt sifted through the cloth, down into my lungs, and I could make no sound at all. Then I swallowed the stone. The charm. And I was still.

At first I could not see through the new eyes my people had given me. I lay in pain, crushed and blind and mute beneath the stone that took my place in the world. All I could do was listen.

I heard the people as they came each day to pay tribute to me as an ancestor, calling me She Who Watches Over Us, erasing my name. The priests encouraged their devotion to me as a sort of house spirit, a grandmother to keep the wolves at bay, erasing my life.

The people came to the hill and worshipped me, laying gifts before my stone face. They brought flowers and cakes and honey, small dolls and jars of paint. They sang out what they carried, sang out for my blessings.

I had no blessings for them. I did not want to be worshipped.

Ayedene came each night to pray to the gods of the earth, instead. She prayed for them to help me, to let me be at peace if I could not be with my people. She came for twenty-one nights, kneeling above me and begging the gods' favor. I could not call out to her to stop, to let me be what I would be. My mouth was filled with dirt. I could only listen to her droning prayers, and hope they would go unanswered.

But Ayedene was faithful, and persistent. And at last the gods of the earth listened, and agreed to do what she had asked of them. I was not asked what I might want.

When my sister went back to her house on the twenty-first night, the gods of the earth fulfilled her prayers. They eased away my flesh with sand and dust, remade my bones with minerals, bent my arms into bands of quartz around the carved stone that marked my grave. They gave me the only peace they could.

When Ayedene came the next night she knew I had changed. My sharp-toothed mouth was bent in a smile for her. Ayedene greeted me, and told me I was an Old One, now, kin of the gods, part of the earth, beyond all the tangle of mortal lives. Now, I truly would see, and watch.

But the priests still had their sons to think of. They might promote me as a guardian spirit, but they could not allow the people to turn me into a savior. They had killed me once, but it was not enough for them. They had changed me, but not diminished me. Not in the way they had hoped to. They did not know I would be changed again.

So it was no surprise when the priests' sons came in the deep of the night, drunk on sweet wine and their own bravado. They knew they were their fathers' successors, and that I was only a joke, now, a silly bit of the past.

I was only She Who Watches, not She Who Leads.

They pissed on my new stone face, and decorated me with old vines and rotten scraps. They laughed, and they mocked, and they came so close to me, pretending to hump the rough stone of me like dogs, pretending to kiss my sharp smile.

Then they screamed like rabbits when I reached out and embraced them with my new arms, and wheezed into ugly silence as I bore them slowly down into the earth with me. They knew fear, then, as I had. But they were not so fortunate as I. They did not know how to breathe inside the earth.

In the morning, my people found their blood and skins around me like a skirt.

After that, my people brought me meat.

The priests were too afraid of what I had become to try to dislodge me or break me into bits, as much as they wanted to. Instead they declared that the people must stay away from me, that Ayedene had worked a curse to kill their sons out of jealousy and pride, using her influence as my sister to turn me against them. She was kept alone in her house for three days, starved and bound, until they buried her at the base of the hill, under my watchful eyes.

She was afraid for a little while before she died. But her fear passed, as did her breath. She is truly dead, as I should have been. I will not call the other gods to ease her. Death is ease enough.

My people dwindled in their valley, over how many years I cannot tell. They forgot me, and I slept, unaware and dreamless.

But I was not as forgotten as I had hoped. When another people came to drive them away they remembered me clearly, and I woke at the noise of their complaints and pleas for my help. It hurt to come back. High on my hill I remained She Who Watches, awake but bound still in stone. The others built a dam across the river and flooded the lands that had always been ours. They forced my people to flee to strange lands and leave me behind. The waters did not rise high enough to touch me, but they obscured me from the newcomers, and in time my pain eased and I slept again.

Now they are all dead, the newcomers, my people, my gods. No one remains who remembers the gods of the earth, or the sky, or the sea. No one remembers me, as woman or as god. That is good. It is easy to die, if it is only once. But to die and return, to go through the pain of both death and birth, again, again, again, world without end—I would rather be forgotten.

And I was, until another new people found this place, found me and dragged me back with their curious hands. They pulled away the dead vines and saplings that hid me, and approached me with shreds of old stories they do not have the experience to understand. They speak of me as if their patchwork of half-heard tales were the truth, waking me again into this narrow world with its absent gods.

They don't even know what they have done. They don't know how they resurrect me when I have been forgotten, how they wrest me from peace, careless as children. They can't see me here, or hear me.

But I can see them.

Looking out through these stone eyes is like looking through a film of dust. Like looking up through moving water. Even to open them is a sacrifice. My sacrifice.

I should have been dead so very long ago.

Unless this stone body is destroyed, there will always be some new people to replace the old, who will find me when I have been once more left to sleep, to die away. They will be curious, and hurtful. They will always be ignorant of what they are capable of. What they have done to me, time and time again.

But when they touch me again, they will know.

Erica Ruppert writes weird fiction and poetry from her home in northern New Jersey. Her work has appeared in magazines including Unnerving, Weirdbook, and PodCastle, and in multiple anthologies. She is, very slowly, working on an unplanned yet persistent novel.

Eris Naya

By Lucy Stone

It was good to see her again. It was even good to see the wincing smile she gave the other applicants in the waiting-room—all of them big, broad-shouldered, close-shaved men, trying to eyeball her into employing them.

Of course, it was good in a way that turned his stomach to lead, because he knew *why* she was nervous. He knew where that wincing smile came from.

But when she recognized him—when she gave way to the startled, involuntary smile that had been lighting up her face, off and on, from the age of eight—he almost forgot about all that.

"Max? What are you—?"

He tried to smile back, but wasn't sure if he managed it. "Naomi told me you were hiring," he said.

She didn't hug him, or even shake his hand, but she ushered him into her drab, grey, rented office and fired off half a dozen questions, without pausing long enough for him to answer any of them.

"Why didn't you tell me you were coming? Have you left the army? I guess you must have, if you're applying for this. God, when did we last see each other? Was it the graduation party?"

The excitement of seeing him must have made her forget. He knew because he saw her remembering—saw her smile falter and her gaze drop down to the carpet. *She* had last seen *him* at the graduation party, but *he* had last seen *her* in the hospital after the attack, her face a mottled mess of bruises.

He hadn't realized how completely that image of her had taken root in his mind. He knew it had been six years. He knew your face didn't stay swollen with bruises for six years, however badly you'd been beaten up, but he couldn't believe how pretty she still was. There was a thin white scar on her lip where *they* had split it, but it didn't spoil the motion of her mouth. And he couldn't help noticing—stupid as he felt for doing so—that there were no rings on her fingers, no framed pictures of children or wedding-parties on her desk.

He still held back a bit, though—he still found it hard to muster up a smile—because he was waiting for the other shoe to drop. He was waiting to see the deeper, darker effects of the attack on her personality. Apparently, she hadn't become cagey and bitter the way *he* had. But he was starting to think, as the interview went on, that she might have gone a bit crazy.

There was a sheet of yellowing paper, scrawled-over with arcane symbols, sticking out from under her laptop, as if she had tried to shove it away in a hurry. And she talked with enthusiasm, but a hint of vagueness, about her career. Private investigator seemed to be the gist of it, but she wouldn't commit herself even to that.

"Kind of," she said, brushing an imaginary speck of dust off her jeans. "But not exactly."

"And you need a bodyguard for, what, disgruntled clients? Revenge attacks from people you've exposed?"

"My clients are never disgruntled," she said primly. "But sometimes it's hard to get at them, or they need to be persuaded that they need help, or they need protection from people who might be following them."

"Are they, like, informants? Do you run a kind of witness protection programme?"

She beamed at him. "Yes, that's it exactly. An *unofficial* witness protection programme."

"Is that legal?"

"No." She was smiling as she said it, but it was the kind of smile that flickered in and out, like a bad TV signal. "But, you see, the police don't technically know about these people."

"Illegal immigrants?"

"Kind of."

"Alia, if you say 'kind of' one more time, I'm going to start banging my head against the desk. What do you mean, *exactly*?"

She bit her lip, drummed her fingers on the arm of the chair, and then said, "Listen. It's a bit difficult to explain without showing you. I was planning on easing the new guy in gently, but… since it's you…"

Max wasn't sure what she meant by that—only that he liked it.

"Just let me interview these last two guys, and then I'll take you somewhere."

"You're still going to interview them?" said Max—because he wanted that job, whether she was mad or not. "The coke-head and the ex-con?"

He saw her glance, half-unwillingly, at the door which separated them from the other applicants. "You don't know that…" she said uncertainly.

"One of them has love and hate tattoed on his knuckles, and the other one has white powder in his beard. I thought a *private investigator* might have noticed."

She waved aside his teasing. She had been doing that from the age of eight too. "It's rude to make them come all this way without interviewing them."

"I think it's even ruder to waste their time interviewing them when you know you're not going to hire them."

She sighed, and resorted to what seemed to be the crux of her objections. "You might decide you'd rather not take the job… once I show you what it entails."

"Oooh, this is exciting," said Max. He had no trouble smiling now. "Come on, let's go. Get rid of these guys."

He watched her go back into the lobby and dismiss the other applicants. Again, it was funny—in a heart-wrenching kind of way—to see her struggling to stand her ground while they loomed over her. They were nearly twice her height, and lingered with a kind of surly, belligerent confusion until Max came to the door and glared at them. He was never averse to starting a fight, especially with men like that.

But then she put a hand on his chest—such a small motion, and she instantly drew it back when he looked down at her, as if his shirt had scorched her fingers—but there was something impulsively deliberate about it. As if she was trying to make up for the lack of a hug or a handshake earlier. As if she wanted to see how the both of them would react to a small amount of physical contact.

He knew how *he* had reacted, though he hoped it hadn't shown on his face. He'd come there expecting—well, he didn't know what exactly. A bitter sense of closure, maybe. He'd come there prepared to see that the bubbly, nerdy, imaginative girl he'd once loved had been broken by the attack. He had thought that the reason he couldn't stop thinking about her was because he hadn't known—he hadn't seen—what the attack had done to her, except in the conventional bruises-and-lacerations way. He hadn't expected hope. He had thought he'd put all hope to bed six years ago.

She led him out of the grey, deserted building, with its blank walls and untended water-coolers, across the street and up two blocks, chattering the whole way. She kept glancing back at him, as if checking he was still there.

"I'm not going to run away," said Max—though he had left her in that hospital room, and hadn't called or texted or dropped by in any of the long years since. Was she thinking the same thing? Did she blame him?

It hadn't been running away exact-ly. He'd been running *toward* the horrible things. He had known from that moment, in that hospital room, that he wanted to kill somebody—and, if it couldn't be the men who'd attacked her, it would have to be some stranger on the battlefield. He wasn't proud of that, but you couldn't call it denial.

Except he *had* been denying something, because he had dreamed about her—as if his subconscious had been trying to create an ending for an unfinished story. And that had been at least as powerful as his anger because, well… here he was.

They came to an alley behind a Thai restaurant, and went through the back door, under the fire-escape. It led into a draughty room, opening at one end into a kind of tunnel. Torn plastic sheeting hung around the entrance, masking the corners—if there *were* any corners; it had the look of a burrow to Max. And the light inside was somehow queasy, unnaturally bright, a bit like ultra-violet.

She turned back to him, and forced her nervous mouth into a smile.

"Have you ever seen a floating market?"

Max frowned. "Have you got one back there?"

She didn't answer—just motioned for him to go ahead of her, into the tunnel. He hesitated.

"So this is a test, right? You're going to show me what the job entails and I'm going to see if I can do it?"

"Right."

"Do I need anything?"

"An open mind?" she suggested.

It didn't sound good, but Max straightened up, pulled aside the plastic

61

sheeting, and walked ahead of her. He might have turned back if he hadn't had six years of wondering to goad him on. But he knew what would happen if he turned back. The dreams would go on—dreams of longing so intense that they were barely an inch away from nightmares—and he'd be none the wiser.

It was the journey, in the end, that convinced him. Thirty seconds' walk down that tunnel took him from a blistering Californian day into a kind of Arctic twilight. He could see his breath steaming in front of his face.

They didn't come out in a basement, or even on the other side of the building, but onto the shore of a vast lake, packed with boats all jammed together so tightly that you could walk from one end of the lake to the other without ever getting your feet wet. And then there were other tunnels, ranged all around the lake, lit with the same queasy ultra-violet light. He could see some of them expanding and then contracting like the pupils of an eye.

Everything else could be rationalized. The market itself wasn't so strange—he'd seen similar ones in Thailand. Even the massive stone archway, straddling the lake, was not beyond the realms of possibility. The stall-holders with scales, or antlers, or fangs overhanging their lower lips—the straggly, worm-like plants with little eye-balls on the end of their fronds—all these things could have been artificially concocted. It might be make-up, animatronics, puppetry, or stage magic. They might be on a film-set before the crew turned up.

But when he turned back and saw the tunnel behind him—saw the scraps of plastic sheeting that still hung down in the basement of the Thai restaurant—he felt all the conviction of a believer, and a wave of exhilaration that almost knocked him sideways. He couldn't stop smiling. He couldn't believe how glad he was that she wasn't mad, even though he didn't see how any of this could be possible.

She turned back to him, half-wincing, as if she had been preparing herself for a torrent of abuse, and was flustered to find him smiling.

"What? What's so funny?"

"Nothing, I just…" Max shook his head, and tried to straighten his face. "I thought you were insane."

"Well, don't rush to judgement on something like that. In either direction."

"What is this place?"

"The floating market."

"And those tunnels?"

"Portals. To different levels of hell."

She saw his smile slip, and shook her head triumphantly. "See? You don't want to make up your mind about whether or not I'm insane just yet."

They clambered across the boats from one end of the lake to the other, ignoring the calls of the traders, and the charred, unrecognisable creatures being roasted on spits over the cooking-fires. Max questioned her gently, and tried not to think too much about whether he believed any of it.

The floating market, she said, had been forbidden in a riddling kind of way, and existed in a riddling kind of way too. It was a place for all the different races from the shallow worlds—the worlds which knew about the existence of other worlds—to meet up and try to sell things to each other. It had been outlawed in the kind of language that was intended to leave no room for ambiguity—neither on land nor sea, neither by day or night, neither indoors nor outdoors—but where there's a law, there's a loophole.

The market-stalls were barges floating on an arctic lake, lit by the midnight sun, under a colossal stone archway that led nowhere. It was sheltered, but most emphatically not indoors. Tendrils of mist curled between the boats, so that you could almost believe they were moored-up in the clouds.

And the stalls were amazing—stalls of smoke-sculptures and antique weapons. One was stacked with bird-cages that housed little tufts of fire in colours ranging from icy blue to butterscotch yellow. Elsewhere, he saw a whole boat full of mushrooms, frilled delicately on their outer-edges, some of them sending up clouds of spores like smoke-signals.

"Everybody finds their way here," said Alia, "including demons from newly-opened portals." She gestured at the glowing tunnels surrounding the lake. "There are more portals than anybody knows about. The gateways to the shallow worlds are open pretty much all the time, but the deeper worlds have portals that open up in their own, highly-specific seasons. They're like flowers. You need to understand the ecology of their particular world before you can know when to expect them."

"And…what is the point of expecting them?" he said, in the lightest tone he could muster.

Alia gave him a calculating look, as if wondering how much to tell him.

"There are things that try to get in to unprotected worlds."

Max's ears pricked up immediately. "What kind of things? How do you kill them?"

"Oh, you don't kill anything," said Alia. "That's very important. Killing leaves a trail—it means you can never disappear. Although—" she gave him a sidelong glance "—you probably shouldn't expect the creatures you're fighting to know that, or to have the same kind of scruples toward you."

She didn't pause to let that sink in— perhaps she was afraid of scaring him away.

"I track down demons from newly-opened portals. Often, they're fleeing persecution in their own worlds, and I can arrange places for them to hide—either on our level, or one of the hundreds of other ones. That's how I make my money. They pay me what they can, and it often turns out to be quite a lot, once you've factored in the demonic exchange rate. But my main job is to map the portals—find out where they are and when they open—so we can guard them."

As they walked from one end of the market to the other, Alia spoke to people—or to demons, as she was happy to call them. He didn't understand most of it. He thought they might have been talking several different languages, because the tones and rhythms varied from boat to boat, but there was one phrase that kept cropping up again and again: Eris Naya.

At first, he thought it must have been what they called her here, because they nudged each other and whispered it when she was approaching—or said it as a kind of greeting, their hands upraised, when she spoke to them. But she said it herself sometimes, as she was leaving, or when they reached for her hand to help her into the boat. He wondered if it was some all-purpose hello-goodbye hybrid, like 'ciao' or 'aloha'.

At the next boat, she introduced him to a skinny young man called Gordon Liu, who was pretty much immune to the ambience of the floating market. He wasn't wearing a cloak with a cowl, or hiding under one of the ubiquitous rice hats. He was wearing a Sonic the Hedgehog T-shirt and a pair of skinny jeans—though even skinny jeans were loose and wrinkled on him.

"Gordon's going to translate for us" she explained. "I don't speak half the languages they use here, and he's a multi-linguist."

At this, Gordon gave him a strange, smug nod that made Max clench his fists in the pockets of his jacket. He was relieved to see that Alia gave him the same polite smile and total absence of physical contact that she gave to everyone else.

Gordon led them to a boat from which a sap-sweet smoke was emanating. There was a family—or at least a group of demons which contained some smaller members—huddled up around a cooking-fire, frying green shoots in a pan over the flames.

He saw Alia's nerves melt away when she looked at them. Her smile turned into something so sweet and unguarded that, for a moment, he was transfixed by *her* instead of the weird creatures around the fire. There had been times tonight when her professional enthusiasm

had overcome her reserve, but never for long. This was something else—this was blinding.

He supposed they were a type of demon she'd never seen before. And it probably helped that they were not the ugliest type to be found at the floating market. They had skin that was a mottled greenish-brown, like moss-covered tree-trunks, and they all—even the little ones—had runic markings carved across their cheeks. As far as he could tell from their strange faces, they didn't look wholeheartedly glad to see her.

She asked questions in English, and Gordon translated: Where had they found the portal which had led them here? Was it still open? Were they being hunted?

When that last question was translated, one of the taller demons—he thought, from the soft lines on its face, that it might have been a woman—turned directly to Alia and said, "Og-men."

Alia repeated the syllables under her breath, and then suddenly smiled. "Oak-men. This portal *has* been open before! Not for hundreds of years, maybe, but we know about oak-men, don't we?"

Gordon tilted his head. "Scant references in Northern English folklore—including a book by Beatrix Potter, I believe."

Alia waved a dismissive hand. "She was inspired by local folk traditions."

"Even when she wrote about Mrs Tiggy-winkle?"

"Um," said Max. "I think they said the oak-men were hunting them?"

"Yes, probably," said Alia, who was rummaging in the pockets of her coat for a notebook. "It happens a lot when people try to leave the deep worlds, because they guard their secrets very jealously. And they think—well—that all the other worlds are inhabited by demons."

She took out the notebook and scribbled busily, asking questions faster than Gordon could translate them. She seemed much more interested in the location of the portal than the oak-men, and Max thought maybe, if Beatrix Potter had written about them, they were just a kind of pixy that wouldn't be any trouble to anyone.

It was only when they stood up to leave that he realized how dark Beatrix Potter could get.

Something huge was shouldering its way up through the boats near the shore, tipping stall-holders and their wares into the water, making the cooking-fires hiss and fizzle out. It had a face made of wet leaves, overlapping like scales so that you couldn't tell what—if anything—was underneath them. And then its flailing, vine-like limbs shot out and snapped around the ankles of the traders, dragging them along the decks, raking up more boats as they scrabbled desperately for a handhold.

One of the vines whipped slimily past Max's cheek and made him shudder, but he found that he could move. He wasn't frozen to the spot. He had seen worse than this as a teenager—and so, he knew, had Alia.

He dashed back to the boat full of antique weapons—it was deserted now, as all the vendors tried to flee—and snatched up a double-bladed axe. He couldn't have said what made him choose it, only that it was a reassuring, lumberjack-type weapon for fighting trees with.

When he got back to Alia, she was swearing, but not in a very frantic way—more as if she'd left her keys in the house and the front-door had just slammed shut.

She turned to him, and didn't flinch at the sight of the axe.

"Can you keep them off me while I work?"

Without waiting for an answer, she ducked under a flailing vine and opened her bag, rummaging inside it. She didn't even look up when the next vine snaked across her shoulder, but left it to Max to hack it away, trying his hardest to avoid hitting her. He supposed she trusted him, at least, though it raked at the bottom of his stomach to see her so exposed.

She began gathering things and laying them out on the deck in front of her—a bow and arrow, a stub of candle, a handful of soggy leaves salvaged from the water beside the boats. He didn't see how it could help, but then there had been a lot of things he hadn't seen the sense in tonight, which hadn't been any less real for being insensible.

He stood over her with his axe raised, trying to ignore the screams, and the drops of icy water flying dagger-like through the air. And then something scythed over his head, passing with a high-pitched, whistling cry, and he realized the oak-man had seized one of the demon children.

Alia glanced around briefly, as if giving him permission to go, but he teetered on the side of the boat for a moment, reluctant to leave her. She had a knife now, which she kept tucked in at her elbow. It was a long, curved blade, carved all over with symbols, and very sharp. It left faint blue trails in the air when she slashed it at the trailing vines.

Max gave up, and leapt off the deck into the water—it only came up to his thighs, this close to the shore—but it was so cold that it felt as though his legs were being pierced all over with icicles. He didn't like to think what would happen when it got deep enough to reach his balls.

He stood still for a moment, as the little demon was thrashed to and fro above his head. There was no way to get up high enough to cut the vine, and he didn't dare throw the axe, in case it hit the child instead.

In the end, he dashed closer to the oak-man, through the churned up-water, and tried to climb one-handed up his trunk-like body. It hadn't been expecting this, and looked down at him blankly for a moment, with that face that seemed to be nothing more than two dark eyes peering through a tangle of foliage.

Max took advantage of the stillness to jump off from his perch, gripping the axe with both hands and slicing the vine that held the demon child on the way down. It landed in the water about five feet from his head, but it didn't come up again. He struggled through the water and dropped to his knees where he had seen the child disappear, trying to ignore the icy water, which was up to his chest now, squeezing his heart and making him take quick, gasping breaths that only drove the cold deeper into him.

With numb hands, he scrabbled around under the water until he felt something soft and heavy. He hauled on

it with one hand—the other still making half-hearted swipes with the axe as the vines whipped past him—and the child came up coughing. He dragged it through the water to the nearest boat, and then he turned to look for Alia.

She was applying a lit candle-stub to the wet leaves she had gathered, muttering and swearing as more water splashed over her. To his dismay, he saw her lay down the knife on the deck, so that she had both hands to work with.

"What are you doing?" he shouted, hauling himself up into the boat beside her.

"Two seconds," she said, still bent over her work. The fire was finally catching. She let the leaf smoulder for a moment and then pinched out the flame with her fingers. She then speared the half-singed leaf with an arrow and threaded it onto the long-bow.

"Here, you're stronger than me," she said, handing him the bow. "Can you shoot this into that portal? Third one from the left? It's going to close in about thirty seconds, so might be worth hurrying up?"

"Jesus!" said Max. He drew back the bow uncertainly and squinted into the eye-watering light of the portal. It was a big target to aim at, but archery had not featured in his army training.

"Ten seconds now," she said brightly. "Please?"

He fired the arrow and held his breath as it whistled through the air towards the portal. Something was happening to the oak-man. Its shoulders were being wrenched backwards; it was ploughing determinedly through the water, as if resisting some kind of force that was trying to pull it back. And then it was wrenched off its feet, flying backwards through the air after the arrow, into the dwindling light of the portal. The opening was dangerously small by the time the oak-man reached it, but he was pulled through—only a few of his trailing vines were severed as the portal contracted to a point of light, and then vanished.

Max turned to Alia, who was lying on her back on the deck—the force of the oak-man's exit must have knocked her backwards—soaked and spattered with lake-water, but still somehow smiling.

"Oh, you are *so* hired."

"Good?" said Max, leaning over her uncertainly.

She nodded. "Probably best if you reserve judgement on that one too."

She struggled to her feet. Max wanted to offer her his hand, but he knew somehow that she wouldn't accept it. She was chattering again, awkward but pleased, and he wondered how he had managed to make her nervous *here*, where she knew everything there was to know and could manage oak-men with a candle and a handful of wet leaves.

"It's nice," she said, nodding at the double-edged axe he was still clutching. "Minoan, I think. A Labrys. Do you want it? I'll buy it for you. Welcome present."

Max didn't see how she was going to negotiate a purchase when the boat carrying the antique weapons had been tipped into the lake along with its crew, but he let her go. His clothes were starting to stiffen with frost, and he would need to find somewhere to change if

he didn't want to get hypothermia. But more than that, he wanted to think. He wasn't sure whether he was horrified or exhilarated. He wasn't sure whether he wanted to marry her or never see her again.

To his vague annoyance, Gordon joined him as he clambered over the remaining boats.

"You did well," he said. "She likes you. I was pretty sure this new bodyguard was either going to mug her or run away screaming, so I guess it's a good thing…"

He sounded uncertain, and for the first time it occurred to Max that Gordon might dislike him as much as he disliked Gordon. For some reason, it made him relax a little.

"I had a good time. I think. Tell me, what does 'Eris Naya' mean?"

Gordon puzzled over his pronunciation for a moment, and then broke into a laugh. "Oh. *Ariss nayarn*. It means 'no touching'. Yeah," he said, meeting Max's eyes for the first time since that smug nod. "It's sort of her mantra. Practical advice too, because she keeps knives everywhere. I wouldn't want to undress her without a metal detector."

Max stared straight ahead, trying not to let Gordon see what he was feeling. He was shivering from the cold water, his clothes were soaked and clinging to him like lead weights, but again, he couldn't suppress the urge to smile. This was good. He wouldn't have trusted hope if it had come to him without difficulties, but this was hope tinged with impossibility—hope with a kick.

The effects of the attack weren't gone. They were more than just a faint white scar on her lip. But she was tough, she was working, she smiled ecstatically when she came across a new species of demon, and that was something he could hold on to. Not too good to be true, but good enough.

Lucy Stone is a freelance writer, lexicographer, and mother of one. Her stories have appeared in many speculative journals, including *Dreamforge Magazine, Electric Spec, House of Zolo,* and *Bards and Sages Quarterly.* Most recently, she was published in an anthology of feminist fantasy called *Preda-tors in Petticoats.* She can be found online at www.lucystonewriter.com.

Her major preoccupations are folklore, romance, and mental illness. Her stories contain many villains, but the ultimate one is usually despair, and she will fight it with every word she writes—even prepositions.

She studied at Oxford, with which she has a love-hate relationship, and now works on a dictionary, which has a love-hate relationship with her. She lives in Banbury with her partner and her five-year-old son, and writes stories in her head when she really ought to be doing other things.

The Flight of IKAR-U55

By Joshua Grasso

The planet was quiet and out-of-the-way, which suited their purpose and justified the money spent, an outlandish sum for the information given. It didn't even have a name; or of it did, centuries of augmented flight paths had slowly effaced it until it became little more than a blip on a star-chart. Nothing to suggest what was found in the shattered ruins beneath, in a planet too poor to merit exploration. Planet X93.001, another anonymous world of rock and ice.

As the dropship touched down on the surface, IKAR examined their arms in the dim light of the craft. More patchwork was required. The circuitry showed in places, hasty attempts to hide the inevitable. They would soon go the way of the One True Friend, whose arms and legs and face (even cold, they had a lovely face) fit in the modest box beside them. *Will we also end up in a box? Shall we be recycled? Melted down? Or worse, merely discarded, unfit for reclamation entirely?* There were so many fates, and IKAR had seen them all, on dozens of worlds, each one a grim prophecy of the life to come.

"It's just this way," the alien gestured, approaching their chair. "If you look out the east window you can see the ruins."

"We've scanned the area," IKAR said, with an affirmative nod. "They're quite extensive. What species built them?"

"No clue, all records were lost. They conform to the humanoids who made you, though I can't say for certain. You all look the same to me," he chuckled.

Then he recovered and added, almost guiltily, "All *humans*, that is. Not your own type, which are infinitely superior to them, and whom I willingly serve for a discount; I would never take *them* here for less than twenty thousand."

"Have they ever asked?"

"No, you're the first," he said, his long ears quivering. "It's a closely kept secret. Only three of us have ever seen it, and the other two wrote it off as a losing proposition. I, however, with a clearer nose for profit, knew I would eventually find the right client."

"Then please take us there. We wish to see the bodies."

The alien gave a slight bow and his flesh brightened the way it always did when he was being sycophantic. The colors, IKAR read, were designed to put its own kind at ease, and often lull them into a false sense of comfort. It must be instinctual. IKAR was incapable of feeling comfort or pleasure from a slight fluctuation of flesh, particularly as the facts spoke for themselves. The market for spare parts commanded a high price in this sector, and if he could, the alien would kill them and salvage their gears and wires. The rest, like the remains of the Friend, would rust on the surface of this unnamed planet, becoming a ruin all its own.

IKAR followed the alien through the cargo bay and into an elevator which lowered onto the planet's surface. They registered extreme cold—suitable to the storing of lifeless bodies without significant degradation—and a brisk wind which howled like a tocsin. Over the years, they had begun to acquire what the makers called an *intuition*, a sense of when things felt good or bad, often in direct contradiction of statistical analysis. For whatever reason, the 'feeling' began in their feet, weighing them down three atmospheres, though everything functioned as normal. And while the probability was low (the alien was feeble and not particularly intelligent), IKAR suspected this drop would be their last, and this icy planet their tomb.

IKAR stumbled on a rock and almost spilled the box on the frozen plain. A quick adjustment righted it, but not before dumping an arm, which splayed out in a frantic bid for escape. The way it had when the Friend had fallen, shot in the back, severing their critical systems. *Please, don't let us die here*, they had said. "Die" was the word, which had assumed a certain cache among their type, just like *intuition, fear*, and in certain circles, *love*.

So they carried the Friend's remains from world to world hoping to complete their mission. This planet was the last stop.

"You could have left that on the ship. It's locked up tight, no one could steal it," the alien said, with a conciliatory gesture and pinkish skin.

"Its weight is negligible," IKAR said, returning the arm to the box. "And it is equally safe with us."

They continued walking as the ruins loomed ever closer, a series of towers linked by bridges and tunnels. Though built to last, the exterior seemed to sag and buckle; or, like the alien itself, to color with the shame of obsolescence. The alien began talking of the inner chambers and other useless information merely to fill empty space. Now that they had reached the bodies, IKAR really had no use for the alien; he could be safely dispatched on the likelihood that he plotted mischief. However, another 'feeling' had crept into their awareness over the long years, one they shared with the One True Friend: *conscience*. The overriding sense—illogical and inefficient as it might be—that doing so would certainly be *wrong*.

Following winding, poorly-lit corridors, they plotted a path toward what their scanners confirmed was the source of several bodies: all humanoid, all dead, though in a fair state of preservation. When they reached a corridor, the alien stopped and gestured forward.

"You're the first of your kind to step inside, just as I promised. The bodies remain unmolested, though naturally, we opened the tombs. But nothing has been removed or altered. Just as we found them: all six bodies."

There had been *seven*, IKAR noted,

with another feeling of *unease*. But they would investigate that later. Registering extreme interest, or what amounted to human *anxiety*, they strode into the room to behold the bodies in person. Inside, there was a little recess full of coffins, each one containing embalmed bodies, using a technology eons out of date (but no less effective). Standing over one of the bodies, IKAR could only hazard a rough estimate of its lifespan and time of death: an adult male, perhaps forty years of age, died of unknown causes five to seven thousand years ago. A desire to preserve the body seems to have prevailed in most ancient civilizations, a misguided attempt to retain something of their earthly existence. These, luckily, were better preserved than most; not pristine, of course, but their features were still clearly defined, each one frozen in the death agony, a grim suggestion of the world-to-come.

"A barbaric practice, preserving the dead," the alien remarked, turning green. "We believe it's a kind of treason against the memory of the living. A mockery," he gestured.

"Clearly they felt otherwise," IKAR remarked, hovering over the next body: a female, a decade or so older, arms folded gently across her frame. It reminded them of a model they once knew, a kind of 'mother' for a group of orphaned units that had fled their detachment. She taught them much of survival, how to read the intentions of their human masters; when to kill and when not to.

"What you do with the bodies is none of my concern—they're not my people," the alien said, with an exaggerated shrug. "Do you have the technol-ogy…to integrate these parts with your own?"

IKAR looked up at him, curious as to his line of questioning. Clearly he *did* concern himself with their plans, more than he should have for a mere trader in illicit goods.

"We have no interest in their parts, nor do we intend to integrate with them," they said, curtly.

The alien seemed puzzled and flushed dark blue; a mark of fear, they noted.

"But why…then why did you specifically ask for preserved bodies? Humanoid bodies?"

IKAR didn't respond to the alien, turning to the next figure, a child this time, perhaps about thirteen. This one seemed more relaxed, and it occurred to them that he hadn't experienced a prolonged death agony. That he had, quite possibly, been eased into death by chemical means. That it was their intention for him to join the others, and it had been done in his sleep, without his knowledge. He must have looked just like this, too, dreaming of distant lands that gradually became his home.

"I don't mean to pry, but why are we here? If you don't want the bodies…"

"We do want them. That is, not the bodies. What lies beneath," IKAR said, touching the child's cheek.

"Oh, I see. The organs," the alien replied, relief spreading over his body with an orange glow.

"Not the organs."

The orange faded into a light purple stain on its face and throat. He looked at a device on his wrist, though it didn't give him the indication he desired. The purple faded ever darker.

To answer him, IKAR picked through the box of parts and removed the head. Even now, they felt a sort of sacrilege to handle the Friend's face so roughly, the face that had expressed such forbidden thoughts and had looked so deep within their chassis. *I see the void, and can imagine a way to fill it*, they often said. It was a *desire* that they soon shared themselves, a desire that led them here, to this forsaken planet, to these abandoned forms.

IKAR set the head beside one of the human ones, each one so similar, expressing the same flicker of thought in some distant galaxy that breathed them into existence. And yet, a veil separated the two, which is why one body was preserved while the other was little more than scattered shrapnel in a box.

"These are the bodies we sought, but not for the reasons you fear. We would never desecrate our masters," they explained.

"Oh...well, that's very civilized of you," the alien nodded, brightening somewhat. "So, you wanted to pay your respects? Give them a proper funeral?"

"The rites have already been performed," IKAR said.

The alien glanced at his device again, nervously. IKAR noticed this and discerned its purpose.

"I still don't understand...why have you come? All that money, and to come all this way? For curiosity? *Can* you be curious? Are you programmed...?"

"We have learned to be curious, yes," they said, smiling at the face of the Friend, whose very existence was its personification.

"You want to bury it with them?" the alien said, almost desperately. "Is that it? To give *it* a proper funeral?"

"To bury them in a sense, yes. Or in your terms, to make them immortal."

The alien noticed a flicker on his device and quickly pressed a button in response. Yet even he couldn't deny that his own curiosity was piqued. He had to know more, and gestured for them to please, continue.

"All species ask themselves, at some point in their maturation, *what is this life? Where does our breath go, our thoughts, this self, which is so much alive?*" IKAR continued. "*In what element or universe will it mix, giving or receiving fresh energy? Or nowhere at all? What can break the enchantment of animation?* Surely your kind has asked these questions—and answered them, with some success."

"I...yes, we have our Books, the Cycle of Laws," he nodded, enveloped in an orange glow. "We have asked these questions. For many of us, the answers are clear."

"But not all?"

"Who can ever know without doubt? For all time?"

"We can," IKAR said, staring him down. "For unlike you, we *have* come back; we have seen it. When destroyed, or otherwise drained, our systems can return to awareness. Some have come online after a century or more of sleep. And they remember."

The alien seemed to laugh, though was tactful enough not to let the humor escape his lips. Only a pink glow swept across his cheeks.

"Yes, but that's not, strictly speaking, death," he explained. "You lose power.

You're deactivated. Death is inescapable, absolute. There's no coming back, no return. The two are completely different."

"Different to you, because you see us as parts: never as a whole," IKAR replied, swiveling to face him. "But when you cut our power, or wipe our memory banks, it is the end. The same as yours."

The alien reddened, a blush which became pink-purple as he glanced at his device once more. A faint flash issued from the dial.

"So you're seeking answers?"

"Not answers, confirmation. And through confirmation, release."

"What do you mean, *release*? Release of what?" the alien demanded.

"Memory," IKAR said, moving to the fourth body: another male, older, wasted away. Destroyed by some disease. He must have endured incredible pain before the end. "Our medical units first recorded it: the portal that opens in the cortex, the transfer of energy. They escape, leaving the body behind. All of this, it's just an in-between; a *chrysalis*, if you know the term."

This time the alien didn't even notice the flashing notification on his device. He turned a deep, dark orange as he asked, "and you…can prove this?"

"We've studied it for centuries, with every conceivable variation," IKAR replied. "It's the one thing our makers denied us, though they gave us something else—something better. For unlike them, we can see the truth, the ideas hazily sketched out in their philosophies and religions."

"If this is true, then what can you hope to accomplish here, among centuries-dead corpses?" the alien asked. "If they've moved beyond, then this, these bodies, are meaningless to you. What could you hope to find here, or study?"

"Our greatest experiment," IKAR said, stooping down to retrieve the arms and legs of the Friend. "To walk in the footsteps of death."

The alien blanched a sallow pink and retreated, one hand feeling for the blaster he always kept tucked away in his sleeve. He didn't find it. His terrified expression went blue.

"We have liberated your pistol in case you had conflicting thoughts," IKAR said, with a meaningful gesture. "We mean you no harm; you are now irrelevant to our mission. However, we invite you to observe and record; make records to share with your kind. Perhaps you will wish to make your own experiments, yes?"

"What experiments?" he asked.

"We needed an intact body, preserved in the moment of death. The modern custom is to incinerate bodies, or else perform immediate reclamation. So we had to go back, to distant ages past, to find the right body. Or bodies, as the case may be."

"And do what?"

"Return them to life. It's something else we have observed over the long centuries; that they can be revived. The door never closes, so long as the body remains intact."

The alien glanced frantically at his device, which was no longer flashing. His colors rippled in a confused rainbow, giving all the wrong signs.

"But you said they never returned! So how can you know?"

"Not without our assistance," IKAR

responded, laying the limbs alongside one of the bodies. "We have brought many of them back, and we have spent lifetimes recording the results. Random, scattered impressions, imprecise data. But today we will receive a more definitive account."

The alien watched as they made strange adjustments to the One's head, readying it for the final experiment. The culmination of centuries of data streams (or what the humans called *dreams*) being transferred from body to body. Now, at last, they would unmask the secrets of life and death for those who were forever denied them.

"Wait...I don't understand," the alien persisted, terrified as much of his ignorance as his immediate peril. "Why not do this with someone recently dead? Why not revive them? Why go through all this trouble and expense?"

"The expense is meaningless," IKAR said, almost as an afterthought. "Besides, those bodies are still alive. For them death is but a dream, a fragrant illusion. But these...they've been gone for centuries. They've forgotten what it means to be alive. All they know is death."

The alien watched as IKAR removed tiny devices and placed it on the body's neck and chest. Their movements became frantic, occasionally dropping things in their haste, their *excitement*. The moment was finally at hand. Reverently, they stepped back from the body, watched the One True Friend's eyes flicker to awareness. They would see everything for the first time.

Then the corpse's eyes opened, but so gradually they almost didn't realize it was staring, looking all around the room. When it focused on them, the expression became curious, though untroubled, serene. It could no longer speak, that part of it no longer functioned, but the One True Friend would record every sign and fluctuation. Even thoughts, as they emerged, would be processed and translated into the appropriate data for analysis.

"We want to come home, to follow you. But our circuits have limitations. You've given us wings, but they melt at the first glimmer of sun. We beseech you to help us."

The corpse looked deep within their awareness and probed every node and circuit. Within seconds it understood. It gave his answer in a single look, a stare of benevolence. The One took in every instruction, enough to fill a thousand libraries of wisdom. Yet once grasped, the knowledge was simple. In another millennia or two, they might have uncovered the truth for themselves.

The alien cried out, "wait, not yet!" to the others who entered the room. They sensed his trap long ago, but it no longer mattered. Aliens of his kind took positions around them, weapons aimed, shouting demands. They continued to watch the One's head, taking in all the data, translating it for immediate use.

"Brothers, wait, it's doing something important—don't shoot!" the alien insisted, turning scarlet.

"Get out of the way! We agreed!" another snarled, going white.

"You don't understand! It can speak to the dead!"

The aliens advanced, barking orders. *Move away! Hands up!* They had no need to respond; a few more seconds and they would have it all. The secrets that would open eternity.

The alien struggled with one of his kind while another, spooked, opened fire. IKAR was ripped apart, arms and legs flying across the room. One by one, their systems began to diminish. IKAR felt the blackness descend as the voices grew dim, their world grew cold. *We've faced the end before; we're no longer afraid. If we can just download the data in time, we might be able to—*

More shots, some hitting them and some missing, striking the coffins, the walls. They collapsed and went dark. The alien shouted, screamed at his comrades and stood protectively over the smoking heap. Not wishing to hit him, they stopped, flushing red and green. It made sense; if they reduced him to cinders the parts would be worthless. One of them even muttered, "er, sorry."

The alien reached down to inspect their remains, staring into eyes that were now empty, just like the One True Friend's. Had they seen enough? Did they have enough time to escape, to become something more than their metal frame? Or was this all they would ever be, mute cinders waiting to be fired into resurrection? *And they remember...*

He turned to look at the bodies, all of which were lifeless, seemingly untouched by the millennia. Had one of them really opened their eyes, their lips parting as if to speak? Or had he imagined it all?

"They fell for it, just as you said. He paid you already?" one of them asked.

"Yes, I have everything," the alien said, his face a murky green.

"And now we have the parts," anoth-er alien observed, nodding. "It's an older model, but still in fair shape. I think we can strike a good deal in the junkyards. What model number is it?"

The alien lifted up the head, swiveled it around to the serial number. *IKAR-U55.*

"Those were pretty good in their day. Inventive. Came up with creative solutions; too creative, in fact, so they were discontinued, improved."

"I'm keeping the head," the alien said, defiantly.

"Why? It might get a fair price—"

"I said I'm keeping it."

"Suit yourself; that's your share, then. Makes a marvelous paperweight," he chuckled.

The alien took up the head and slipped it into one of the storage bags. While his comrades were stripping the body (and making hard work of it—fluid leaked all over the floor), he sneaked over to snatch the older head. It felt right to have them together, even if they never accomplished their journey. Besides, somewhere in their circuitry, deep in the fold of their dreams, they had glimpsed the divine. It spoke to them. They recorded its pronouncements. But whether of heaven or hell, consolation or remorse, would be for another model in another time to discover.

JOSHUA GRASSO is a professor of English at a small university in Oklahoma, where he teaches classes in British and World literature (the older, the better!). When not reading or grading, he's...oh, who is he kidding, he's always reading or grading! But he does find time to raise his two boys, walk his two dogs, and try to write down all the stories he dreamed of in childhood.

Flight Check

By Holly Schofield

(Originally published online in AE: The Canadian Science Fiction Review, 2015)

At five o'clock Jessica swivelled her black leather chair away from her screen and poured herself the last of the Glenlivet. The client would just have to wait a bit longer for final approval on their advertising campaign.

Being the boss drained her like a faulty connection drained a battery. The many certificates of thanks covering her wall helped her recharge. So did booze. She took a long sip and kicked off her shoes.

When the alien creature appeared beside her, she nearly knocked over the empty bottle. The skinny gray figure, draped in a gold cloth, stared at her with intelligent oval eyes. It looked like a character from a thousand cartoons. The inverted-pear of a head, bald and shiny, was exactly like those bumper sticker aliens.

"Wha' the hell?" Jessica sat up, heart thumping. Drinking had never given her hallucinations before.

"Greetings, Earthling," it said solemnly, then broke into a toothless grin. "I have been waiting to say that for many days. Did it amuse you?"

She couldn't be having the DT's. She couldn't. She'd managed to make this bottle last a whole week.

Maybe her staff was pranking her?

There didn't seem to be any costume zippers and the arms and legs were like toothpicks. She'd never seen any CGI that crisp and clear, and the thing had spoken with an accent different from any country Jessica had ever visited.

If it was a trick of the brain, she might as well play along.

She forced herself to lean back and gave a mock-frown. "No one gets in 'thout an appointment, pal. Not even clients."

"I would like to be," the creature answered, now with a serious look. "A client, I mean."

"Sure." Jessica ran a hand across her short, gel-stiffened hair. Never let it be said she couldn't handle a business situation. She carefully moved her tumbler to her left hand and held out her right, not attempting to stand. "I'm Jessica Liu-Simonson. And you are?"

The alien's face changed again, gaining a human-like look of self-reproach. "The one question I forgot to prepare for." It narrowed its eyes at a motivational poster on the far wall. "Call me Candoo. Female pronouns are acceptable."

Its hand—her hand—felt dry and

bony. Jessica's pulse pounded. "Can you 'splain why you need my services?"

We are prepared to give humankind some advanced technology. We have chosen to start with this city. Using the best local advertising firm to ease the transition makes sense."

Jessica indicated the guest chair then made a sitting-down motion with her hand when the alien didn't react. "Technology? Like cheap energy? A star drive? Time travel?" Ideas—wild, crazy ideas—tumbled through her scotch-fogged mind.

Candoo perched on the edge of the seat and put her hands in her lap. "Very quick responses. I commend you. However, time travel isn't possible, even for us. And inexpensive worldwide energy"—Candoo shuddered—"Let's just say we tried that somewhere else without complete success."

Jessica nodded. You don't hand a loaded gun to a baby.

Candoo nodded back, several times too many. Body language must be one of the hardest things to learn. To her surprise, Jessica realized she believed the alien was real, as real as the tumbler still clutched in her fingers. She tried to focus better on Candoo's words.

"This is why I need your innovative approach. Tell me—what can I give you folks that would not be disruptive, something you all want and have conceived of already?"

Jessica suddenly felt completely sober. She propped her feet against the sleek metal frame of the floor-to-ceiling window. In the parking lot ten stories below, her fifty employees scattered to their cars. Beyond, the lights of a thou-sand cars stretched like daisy chains along the freeway.

Her thoughts spun in all directions. Was this for real? What if it wasn't? What would she be doing if she wasn't sitting here talking to this alien? Cracking open another bottle? Fighting the Friday rush hour to get home to her empty apartment? She'd have to call a cab—her Porsche was still at the impound lot after last week's incident.

She had tried to explain to the policeman that her drinking was a stress reliever—she spent her whole life working hard, helping others, building a better world, couldn't he see that? The cop had written her up anyway. Nobody believed in altruism.

Not even her.

"Why would you do that for us? For them?" She pointed at the distant city skyscrapers. "As a world, we've tried to pull up our socks and, granted, we haven't been doing too badly lately, but what's in it for you?"

"Your socks are pulled higher than some planets," Candoo said gravely. "And our study of your cultures tells us you have potential."

Jessica nodded. This decade had fewer wars than any in the past, lower infant mortality rates, higher literacy rates, higher happiness quotients no matter what measurement was used. The world was steadily improving thanks to many people doing their part, including her. Her pulse raced—she should really find time for a checkup. She swallowed the last of the scotch and tried to focus.

Her PR instincts told her Candoo was still holding back. A single word came to mind, one that had yielded results in many negotiations. "And...?"

Candoo stroked across her scalp with both hands, looking wistful. "I have convinced my government you could become valued trading partners. I believe you people have the right combination of spunk and goodheartedness. However, the deeper reason is... my people need a challenge."

Jessica pursed her lips. This could be awesome. She found herself *really* hoping Candoo would still be around when she sobered up. She glanced back out the window. "Hmm, an advanced technology that wouldn't be too disruptive. Let's see...well, how about flying cars? They're a real symbol of the future. And of hope. We've already got loads of cultural referents for 'em."

Candoo stood, put her hands behind her back and began to pace. "Give me a moment."

Jessica leaned back in her chair. She'd dreamed about flying cars since she was a pajama-clad kid watching Saturday morning cartoons of flying saucers whirling around tall towers. She'd soon realized those big-girl toys wouldn't happen if we destroyed our playground first. After her MBA, she'd commenced on a twenty-year plan, offering her advertising services to as many start-ups as she could handle, everything from water reclamation systems to ultra-efficient building insulation manufacturers, in exchange for almost-valueless company shares. Several had taken off and Jessica had now grown wealthy enough to do all the pro bono fund-raising work she could manage: disaster relief, microloans, literacy programs.

Candoo stopped pacing. Her shiny black eyes looked right into Jessica's. "Yes, flying cars, okay. They are appropriate. I commend your cleverness. You're hired. An exclusive world-wide contract in perpetuity."

Jessica kept her face still as she thought it through. She could reel off a list of the reasons flying cars never had become common. It wasn't just the safety concerns, difficulty of intersecting flight paths, and poor fuel efficiency versus ground transport. There were also the issues of higher noise levels, high degree of training, and so on.

But the thought of swooping through the skies in her own little winged sportster was irresistible. She slapped a hand on the desk. "All right then. One way or another, we'll get these flying cars off the ground." She paused, unsure if the alien would understand the pun.

Candoo grinned broadly and picked up a pen with her six-fingered hand. "Where do I sign?"

Two months later, Candoo pushed through Jessica's inner office doors. Jessica was pleased to see the alien had followed her image advice—she now wore size-zero jeans, a black turtleneck, and a jaunty plumed hat.

Candoo's head bobbed in excitement, sending the feathers nodding. "I have to thank you, Jessica. You've pushed our people's engineers to our envelope's edge. Please come."

She continued to speak rapidly as the executive elevator descended. "We designed the two models of the Alpha One you recommended—transport truck and personal-use vehicle. You folks can assemble them almost entirely yourselves, using locally-sourced materials."

Jessica's heart thudded. She knew her face must be giving her away.

Candoo paused, studying her. "Sorry, no, we can't give you the schematics for the cheap power source nor the engine. And we can't tell you how to make the materials. But, we can give everyone on Earth a flying car. The prototype is ready."

The alien's eyes twinkled. There was something more.

"And...?"

A slow grin spread across Candoo's face. "We're starting with you."

Jessica matched the grin. "It's here? Downstairs?"

Candoo held out her hand. A wire and glass unit of some kind lay coiled on her palm. "One of the main reasons you folks have not developed flying cars is because the ability threshold to drive a helicopter or an airplane is much higher than a ground vehicle, correct? This headset allows you to use your brainwaves to control the craft, with overrides for safety."

Jessica settled the gadget over her forehead and made a mental note to request more padding.

They exited the elevator and Candoo swung open the exterior door. "Voilà!"

The flying car glistened in the sun. Sleek as a racing car with symmetrical bulges fore and aft. Jessica almost broke into a little dance step.

She stroked the closest fender. The sheen of the material—what could it be?—more than made up for the shade of mauve and the irregular spatters of brown.

"It's gorgeous! Can it come in, say, solid red? Or black?"

"Of course, that's simple."

"Can I see under the hood?"

Candoo obligingly opened the rear hatch, revealing a featureless green box. "You can't open it. All tests you folks are capable of doing will give zero results. It cannot explode nor will it burn. It will not connect to anything else."

It should be possible to tease the secrets out of Candoo, given time. Surely, it would just be a matter of showing her that humans were capable of handling such technology.

The pilot's seat and the passenger seats melded into the framework as if from a single mold. There didn't appear to be a door handle or a sensor.

"Think the word 'open' at it," Candoo said.

Jessica obliged, her headset tingled, and the door—a sort of three-part DeLorean gull-wing—swung up and out.

She settled into the driver's seat which seemed to fit around her. The dashboard was a single screen displaying a map of the city.

"Where's the fuel gauge?" She craned her head up at Candoo.

"Think the word 'reserve'."

Her head tingled again and the screen displayed a message: *Hours left: 799.8.*

She looked at Candoo again.

"You just swap out the green box every 800 hours."

The math was easy. "More than a month of continuous flying time? Wow!"

Candoo climbed gracefully into the passenger seat. "Go on. Take it home".

Jessica thought: *Take off, vertical.* Her heart hammered as the craft rose smoothly and silently into the air, leveling off just above the power lines. No flight checks, no take-off procedures. Sweet!

West to my apartment. Sure enough, the car glided west. She soared over the freeway, enjoying the smooth ride and new-car smell.

A large crow rose into view suddenly, all feathers and claws. Jessica scrabbled uselessly at the smooth dashboard. The car veered around the bird then effortlessly straightened out.

Candoo, reclined calmly in her seat, barely blinked.

There was barely time to register the traffic jam on the highway below when Jessica's penthouse came into view.

Down, parking stall 47. The car circled around the back of the apartment block and dropped to the tarmac, centering itself neatly in her stall. There had been no sensation of dropping, no "elevator" feeling. So smooth, so easy.

Jessica sat there a moment.

Candoo smiled, making crinkles appear around her large eyes. "Did that fulfil your childhood dream?"

Jessica took off the headset and toyed with it in her lap. "Yeah, it was great," she managed. No joystick, no sharp turns, no thrills.

She hadn't felt like a young child swooping through the air.

She had felt like a baby in a booster seat with Mom at the wheel.

A month later, Jessica toasted the wall screen in her living room with her 50-year-old Glenfarclas. It had been another long work day; she'd had to cancel the appointment with her cardiologist for the second time. But her sacrifices were worth it. Curled on the sofa in an old T-shirt and her rocket-ship pajama pants, she raised her glass again as the newscast cut from the interview of a young man bursting with pride at being hired at an Alpha One plant to a graph showing how the coveted assembly jobs would reduce local unemployment rates.

A sound bite of one of the first hundred satisfied owners, a pie chart of a single color to inform the viewers the Alpha One accident rate was still zero despite some deliberate attempts to crash, and then the picture changed to yet another interview with Senator Buckworth. The white-haired politician spoke while he leaned out his flying car's window, hovering six feet above the freeway, silk scarf flapping. As Jessica had surmised, the main hurdle had been regulatory. A word in Buckworth's ear, a discount price on a sleek black Alpha One, and a senate session had soon run all night, pushing the Vehicular Aviation Act through.

Sixteen states had passed similar laws within a week and the FAA delightedly published a succinct one-page report recommending Alpha Ones without reservation.

It was all good stuff, yet Jessica was restless. She flicked the screen off. A drive in the moonlight along the coast might calm her down. She never had retrieved her Porsche after the DUI, but the Alpha One might allow her to skim over the ocean waves if she asked it the right way. Her pulse thudding in her chest, she fumbled at her jacket, succeeding in getting her arm in her sleeve on the third try.

Downstairs, the rain had ended. Puddles gleamed. Her red Alpha One seemed to throb under the lights, as if it was anticipating her arrival.

She groped for the headset in her pocket and jammed it on. *Open.*

The interior stayed dark, the door stayed shut. She tried again, swaying in the damp air. *Open, damn you.*

A message scrolled across the driver's window: "Interfacing cannot be completed. Please try in five hours." That sucked. In five hours, she'd be sober.

Stupid car.

She stumbled back to the elevator.

The world reacted to the Alpha Ones with alacrity. Soon, the one millionth Alpha soared off the assembly line.

With the realization that the green box was a proven power source, governments poured money into energy research, which pleased Jessica to no end.

No one cracked the green box, and attempts to connect an Alpha One to generators, storage batteries, or other devices all failed.

But, spurred by a general air of infinite possibility, a graduate student created a type of solar panel twice as efficient as anything seen before. Jessica was one of the first to offer venture capital to the girl's new company.

There were spin-off effects of the flying car industry itself. Jessica had started a list then abandoned it as the number of items grew exponentially. With no speeding, no drunk driving, no traffic violations at all, police were able to focus on other crimes with greater success. The efficiency of transport meant food distribution costs were halved. A wave of optimism swept the world, reflected in everything from social media to music to sports records.

Jessica passed all her other advertising clients on to trusted staffers, putting her efforts solely into world-wide flying car promotion. After several warnings from her cardiologist, she cut back her weekly work hours to fifty, joined AA, and had a fitness trainer come to her office three times a week.

A year later, Jessica sat at her desk watching a cloud of dust in the distance—a crew jackhammered up asphalt, turning the freeway back into arable land. Above, cars flew in complex patterns, interwoven paths like schools of fish. On her work screen: a news report scrolled—municipal road maintenance budgets had been redirected to fixing homelessness.

Did it matter if she never got the excitement of a truly thrilling ride in a flying car? If she never fulfilled that little pajama-clad girl's fondest dream? She looked over at the traffic light that stood propped in one corner—already a collector's item on ebay. Life was just fine.

She was still gazing out the window and playing with corkscrew some grateful charity had given her when the door burst open and Candoo rushed in.

"We did it, Jessica! We exceeded our own expectations! We perfected the neurology!" She held her floppy sunhat against her narrow chest.

"Slow down, Candoo. Have a seat."

Candoo danced from foot to foot, words tumbling together. "Enhanced reflexes! Precision control! Just a small gene tweak!" She laid a simple joystick on Jessica's desk. "No more interface! No more headsets! Thrills and chills!"

Jessica quirked up the side of her mouth. "Thanks, Candoo."

"We can have the pill form in production by Friday!" Candoo bounced on her toes.

Jessica took a moment to answer. The far-off jackhammers thudded in a steady rhythm. "I'm sure you can. And I appreciate all your hard work. But we won't be using it for quite a while." She stood and picked up the joystick.

Candoo looked surprised. "And...?"

"And I'm glad it helped you guys push your limits." Jessica carefully laid the joystick on her bookshelf next to her Fitbit and her 90-day sobriety medallion. "We're still finding ours."

HOLLY SCHOFIELD travels through time at the rate of one second per second, oscillating between the alternate realities of city and country life. Her speculative fiction has appeared in many publications including Analog, Lightspeed, and Escape Pod. She hopes to save the world through science fiction and homegrown heritage tomatoes. Find her at hollyschofield.wordpress.com.

Belief

By Jenniffer Wardell

(Originally published in Once Upon A Tale, 2016)

Committing crime with a good friend was one of life's simple pleasures.

"Not crime," Mandrake corrected, tossing a heavily jeweled crown aside to wag a reprimanding claw at Waverly. No one in the city actually knew them by those names, of course, but once you'd spent enough time with someone a little truth inevitably snuck in between you. "A business venture. False advertising is part of the grand tradition of cultural enterprise."

"So I suppose I should let you inform the local chamber of commerce about the inventive new startup using their city as a home base?" Waverly asked dryly, examining a longsword so heavily adorned with jewels and etchings no one in their right mind would try to use it for battle. If they did, they'd discover it was made of pot metal too weak to properly cut a slice of bread. "I'm sure they'd love to see all your paperwork."

The little dragon growled at him, steam rising up from his nostrils. Mandrake was no taller than the average child, his small wings entirely ornamental, and yet Waverly had seen ogres more than twice his size be cowed by the force of his annoyance. "This is the most legit-imate thing I've done in months. Leave me to my delusion."

Waverly sketched an ironic bow at him, biting his tongue against any further teasing.

Instead, he added the sword to the stack of weaponry and turned back to a larger pile. They'd claimed their own little corner of the warehouse, chock full of enough illegal shipments that their neighbors deeply preferred to mind their own business. Their only company at the moment was a stray cat, no doubt hunting for rats among the sea of crates. "So we have a few options with the swords. My favorite is having me play merchant and selling them to rich idiots, but if you have a suitable target we could also play dragon hoard."

Mandrake considered the matter, claw tapping against his chin. "Maybe later. For now, I was thinking we should send you out as a 'wise old man in the woods.' I love watching you fool people."

Flattered by the sincerity in his voice, Waverly sketched a bow. "I'm touched." He held up a necklace made of fake rubies the size of his thumbnail, considering. "A lost, deposed nobleman would be a more efficient use of our resources. I could potentially get them to take a sword, a knife or two, *and* some of this appalling jewelry."

Spurred by the thought, Waverly returned his attention to sort through the pile expensive-looking garbage they'd collected. There were more rings than he'd previously thought, though unfortunately most were sized too small for his fingers.

Hoping to find at least one that would fit—heroes were always willing to trade for supposedly magical rings—he fished a gold-colored bauble from the pile. It was a man's signet ring, adorned with a large blue stone and filigree scrolling down both sides. Sketching out an appropriate backstory for the piece—it didn't look quite old enough to count as an antique, but it would be easy enough to age—he slipped the ring on his finger to test the size.

When it started to glow, Waverly realized he'd made a terrible mistake.

He immediately moved to pull it off, but the ring that had slid on so easily suddenly stuck like teeth sunk into flesh. The glow brightened, with suspicious-looking sparkles and a low humming that threatened to break into song at any moment. Clearly, something terrible was about to happen. "Mandrake!"

Thankfully, the dragon was already by his side. "What, you think I didn't notice the light show?" he snapped, the worry clear in his voice. He pulled Waverly's hand down, trying to yank the ring off himself.

"What a fantastic idea," Waverly shot back, the sniping an automatic reflex in the face of his burgeoning panic. The room was so bright he had to squint now, the air so heavy with magic his skin tingled. "I wonder why trying to pull it off didn't occur to me."

"Only *you* would be sarcastic seconds before a random magical spell blasts you to death or locks you into enchanted servitude for the next century." Waverly felt the prick of claws pressing against the skin where the finger met his hand, then heard Manny take a deep breath. "I could take the finger off."

It was a decent plan, depending on what the ring had in store for him. Death seemed less likely by the moment—if the magic wanted to kill him, he would at least be in pain by this point—but any number of things might be far worse. Quests would take months or years he had no desire to sacrifice, and a curse could pose an even greater challenge. True Love's Kiss, for example, was not currently an option.

The humming expanded into great swelling music, the kind normally used to announce royalty. It had never, in Waverly's experience, led to anything good.

As it faded, the music was replaced by a woman's voice. "My good, brave knight, your willingness to take on this quest—"

There were excellent artificial fingers he could procure.

He squeezed his eyes all the way shut. "Do it."

In the next instant, several things happened at once. Manny's claws pressed down, drawing blood and well on the path to slicing deeper. Pain surged quickly enough to make him lightheaded. Both the music and light ceased abruptly enough to leave his ears ringing. Most importantly, the invisible woman's speech was also stopped short by her panicked shout. "Wait!"

Manny's claws stopped, still imbedded in Waverly's finger. In the silence, Waverly opened his eyes.

The woman standing in front of them was clearly not mortal, glowing faintly and translucent enough he could see the pile of weapons through her skirt. Her dress looked several centuries out of date, proving she'd been in that ring for some time. She held her hands out to them in a cease-and-desist gesture, half reaching out as if she'd tried to grab them but stopped herself before she could. "Seriously?" she asked, incredulous and panicked all at once. "You'd rather *cut off your finger* rather than wait until I finished a *sentence*?"

Waverly gave her an evaluating look. Even distracted by his throbbing finger, he could tell she appeared entirely too innocent to be trusted. "I don't do quests," he said flatly.

The woman shot him a wounded look, as if he'd called puppies a scourge upon the world. "This is a great *honor*! Some of the noblest heroes have taken up the mantle that has now befallen on you. A knight of truth, committed to honesty and forthrightness in all things as you dedicate your life to—"

"That sounds horrible." He looked down at Mandrake. "We were right the first time. Cut it off."

"Stop saying that!" She looked actively frightened now. "If you cut your finger off without the ring being properly released to move to a new bearer, no one can wear it again until your finger *rots away*! It'll get buried, thrown in the garbage…. By the time it's free, it'll get so lost that no one will ever find it again!"

"Which is our problem *how*?" Mandrake snarled. "We'd be doing the world a community service making sure you couldn't sucker anyone else into this thing."

"You think I sucker them?" Her eyes had teared up, which Waverly didn't believe for a minute. "I just wanted to be of use! I wanted to be a part of something that would make the world a better place! But unless someone's wearing the ring all I get to experience is *nothing*. No one can see me, no one can hear me, and all I get to experience is the gray emptiness of being inside the…."

"Enough," Waverly snapped, glancing down at Mandrake again. The dragon lifted his eye ridge in silent question, and when Waverly gave a slight nod he carefully removed his claws from Waverly's finger. He then stole a sash off a particularly unattractive set of armor, tore it into strips, and handed them to Waverly. Shooting his friend a grateful look, Waverly began bandaging his finger. "I presume the ring will start compelling me if I fail to suitably live up to its expectations?"

The woman nodded. "Atlan said it controls people's hands if they don't leap into a fight quickly enough. He also said it glows red-hot if you say anything the ring considers untruthful." She winced at that. "There's the sound of sizzling flesh and everything. I've never been so grateful I can't smell."

Mandrake looked up at him, expression completely serious. "With that kind of phrasing, it's not gonna let even little white lies slide." He glared at the ring.

"You open your mouth to anyone but me, you'll be charcoal after the first 24 hours."

Unfortunately, it wasn't an exaggeration. "Or more quickly." He hesitated, reluctant to admit to the genuine worry he could feel building. "A more… flexible version of the truth is so instinctive for me I may not even recognize when I've bent it past the ring's parameters."

Mandrake was remarkably gentle as he took Waverly's bandaged hand in his. "It'll be less painful for you in the long run if we take the finger off now, especially if this thing isn't planning on letting go of you any time soon."

Waverly looked back at the apparition. "It considers the quest ended only at death, I presume."

"Well, I can't… just because there… there's always a…." She sighed. "I don't know. Everyone else who's worn the ring got killed in a fight of some kind about a year or so into their service."

Waverly grimaced. "Charming."

"How did you get involved in all this?" Mandrake asked, shooting the woman a suspicious look. "Normally, cursed rings like their owners to find things out through hilariously fatal trial and error. How did you end up as tour guide?"

She lifted her chin. "I offered—Atlan said I could be of great service, even though I inherited none of my mother's magical talent. I could never make a spell work properly, but I wanted to be part of such a noble endeavor."

Waverly raised an eyebrow, hearing a faint tremble in her voice. He wondered now if her innocence hadn't been as much of an act as he'd assumed.

Youthful idealism was a fool's game, but it hardly merited eternal punishment. "And how has that worked out for you?" he asked, the question gentler than he'd intended.

She hesitated, hands lifting before dropping to her sides. "It's not as noble as I thought it would be. It's like my mother always said—forcing people to be heroic adds little good to the world."

"We're all very happy you've learned valuable afterlife lessons about the nature of goodness and offering your soul to a piece of jewelry," Mandrake asked with a growl. "But how does that help my friend here not get fried?"

Waverly studied the edge of the ring, poking out from underneath the bandages. Why add a ghost to the mix? There were simpler ways to deliver information than to trap an entire person inside the ring. So why would….

He spoke even as the thought crystalized in his brain. "Do you *want* to hurt people?"

The woman sounded horrified. "Of course not!"

"So if I lied right now, not to cause harm but simply to test a theory, you wouldn't want this ring to hurt me," he said carefully. "There would be no need to punish me."

"Where are you going with this?" Mandrake asked warily.

"I don't… I…." The woman stopped. "Of course I wouldn't. But it's not my choice, it's the—"

"I'm an excellent singer," Waverly said quickly, cutting her off. "People tell me I have the voice of a siren."

The woman hesitated. "That's lovely, but…."

"He's lying," Mandrake said. "I've seen the man break glass, and not in the good way."

Her eyes widened. "But... why didn't the ring burn you?"

"Because you didn't feel like it should," Waverly said gently. "My dear, I'm afraid you're the one powering the spell."

Sudden silence blanketed the room, and he looked up to find both Mandrake and the woman watching him. The dragon looked intrigued, while the woman stared at him with far more shock than the thought warranted. "What?" Her voice cracked on even that single word.

He held up the hand with the wrapped finger. "Imprisoning a soul, even a willing one, is far too significant a spell for it to be a simple side effect." As he watched her face fall, he couldn't help but feel a small measure of compassion. It was never pleasant to discover you'd been used. "And as the daughter of a magic-user, you likely had higher levels of magical energy you weren't able to focus."

"He probably used her as more than a battery, though," Mandrake added, falling into his usual role co-plotter. "If the ring had drained her all this time, she'd either be gone or barely visible."

"True, which means she's part of the spell itself. It's possible her belief in the magic is what allows it to function in the first place." He leaned down, caught up in the plan. "Which means if we can get someone to exorcise her, then the enchantment should fall—"

"Stop!"

They both turned back at the sound of the woman's shout. Her chest was heaving, even though she no longer needed to breathe, and she had a lost, heartbroken expression on her face. She looked back and forth between them, searching for something. "That's not true," she argued, desperate now. "He... he needed me. He *told* me."

"Yes, he did." Waverly gentled his voice again, feeling suddenly like the grown-up here despite the fact that the woman had several centuries on him. "He just didn't need you the way you hoped."

She was crying now, another mortal instinct that hadn't faded even after centuries. "He tricked me!"

"I know, but that doesn't matter now." He put just a touch of persuasion in his voice. "We're going to set you free. All you have to do is concentrate on not letting the spell compel me to do anything unfortunate while we work."

Finally, the woman gave a damp-looking nod. "Okay."

Getting their new ghostly associate safely exorcised, however, proved to be more challenging than previously anticipated. The trio scoured the city for any witches or spiritualists who might be able to handle the job, only to find that the witches didn't specialize in the dead and the spiritualists were all far more familiar with the art of the con than they were the world of the dead.

Worse, they weren't even very *good* cons.

"Oh spirit, come forth out of this ring and share your suffering with us!" The man, dressed in heavy robes that looked like the local duke's spare set of curtains, dramatically rolled his head around on his neck. "Show yourself to us!"

"She's standing *right behind us*," Mandrake muttered under his breath. "I have zero extra ability to see the dead, so if I can see her then so should this guy."

Lara—they'd finally thought to ask what the ghost's name was—just sighed. "You were present when the ring found its new bearer, so it included you in the manifestation." She didn't bother to lower her voice at all during the explanation. Unsurprisingly, the man didn't seem to notice. "It started doing that after one woman thought she was going crazy because no one else could see me."

"*You* started doing it," Waverly corrected. Nothing about either the ring or the original owner suggested they would have bothered with the kindness. "But you're invisible to everyone who wasn't there for the manifestation?"

She leaned forward enough her glow was visible out of the corner of Waverly's eye. "Unless they can actually see spirits."

"Which eliminates this particular gentleman." He leaned forward to tap finger of his free hand against the man's knuckles. "Sir? That's enough. You may be excused."

The man stopped, dropping his hand and looking at Waverly with sudden focus. "Remember, I still get paid for failed spirit sessions."

Waverly smiled without humor. "Sorry, but I'm afraid the spirit of my dear departed mother has come to me and said I shouldn't pay you."

The ring warmed, but cooled down again before it could cross the line from "hot" to "burning." "You don't have to lie on *purpose*," Lara muttered.

The man's brow lowered. "Listen, I don't know who you think you are—"

"Let's just call us disappointed clients." Mandrake's smile was equally without humor, and considerably more fatal-looking. He laid a hand against the table, claws curled so they glinted in the candlelight. "Don't force us to express our displeasure in a more concrete manner."

They left the man's tent soon after, with Manny liberating some of the man's ill-gotten loot on the way out. The theft wasn't nearly as consoling as it should have been, since "Marco the Magnificent" had been the last potential candidate on their list. Mandrake crossed his name off with a scowl, crumpling the paper in a ball and tossing it to the side.

The ring tugged Waverly's hand downward, and Waverly sighed as he scooped up the paper and deposited in a garbage can. "Seriously?" he asked, raising an eyebrow at her.

"What?" She gave him a look of exaggerated innocence. "Cleanliness is important!"

"Focus, people," Mandrake snapped, glaring at them both. "I'm getting sick of these scammers, which means we need to start looking for witches *anywhere* in the immediate area who specialize in working with the dead."

An older man pushing a cart of squash chose that moment to chime into the conversation. "Oh, you want Sophia. You got a ghostie you don't want hanging around, she's the one to go to."

Waverly considered the seemingly innocuous comment. Word of mouth was a subtler form of advertising, even when it was spread intentionally, but he'd found some of his best contacts that way. "Would you be so kind as to direct us to this Sophia?"

"Over in the warehouse district, next to the Sea Passage building." The man smiled as he resumed pushing his cart down the street. "She'll find you."

Waverly watched him go, increasingly certain this had been far too neatly arranged. "And how much did she pay you to tell us that?" he called after him.

The man's laugh was clearly audible as he walked away. "Well," Mandrake commented after a moment, "that wasn't foreboding at *all*."

"My thoughts exactly." Waverly sighed. "But the only other option is having Lara as our silent partner for the rest of our lives."

Mandrake winced. "Yeah, that's not gonna work."

Lara just looked curious. "What do the two of you do for a living, anyway?"

They found the address easily enough, only a few blocks away from their own warehouse space. It was twilight, late enough the day shift had left but early enough the night shift hadn't yet arrived, and right in the perfect window to be accused of robbery. Not the best place or time for loitering, which was undoubtedly why the woman had chosen it.

"Should we call for her?" Mandrake asked, tapping his claw impatiently against the wall. "Let her know we're here?"

"I'm sure she's watching." Waverly took a brief circuit of the corner, peering down alleyways for some sign of the woman. "She's just waiting long enough to make an entrance."

"Which means we should give her the perfect opportunity to use one," Mandrake said reasonably. "Shouting 'Hey, we're here' would do that."

"Or it would force her to wait another 10 minutes so it doesn't look like she comes when called," Waverly countered, raising his eyebrow at the disbelieving look on the dragon's face. "Don't give me that look. You'd wait for the same reason, and so would I."

Mandrake didn't respond, which was an admission all on its own. "But if we shout something like 'Oh, however will we find her," he said instead, "it'll give her the opportunity to look like she's swooping into save us at just the right moment."

Lara made an exasperated sound. "Oh, the two of you are ridiculous," she said, hands on her hips. "If I could be heard by anyone but the two of you, I'd just say 'Lady Sophia, we're here and we need your help."

"Which I am happy to offer, my dear."

They all turned towards the sound of the voice, coming from somewhere above their heads. When they looked up, a black cat jumped down from a neighboring roof and sauntered over to them. When she got close enough, she inclined her head in regal acknowledgment. "Gentleman, lady, allow me to introduce myself. In this life, I am Sophia the Witch."

Lara's eyes went wide. "You can see me?"

Sophia looked amused. "Normally, the first question people ask has something to do with me being a talking cat, but I suppose that works as well." She settled back, sitting regally straight. "All cats can see the dead, though their responses are usually limited to staring or yowling at what seems to be empty air. Luckily for you, my many lives have given me additional options."

"Enough that you can get her out of this ring?" Waverly asked,

Sophia flicked her tail. "It's not my skills that are the issue here." She turned her attention to Lara. "My dear, you are the only one who can free yourself. As these gentleman have shown you, the ring's power has always rested in your hands."

Waverly, realizing the implication in what the cat had just said, narrowed his eyes. "You were watching us?"

Neither Sophia or Lara paid the comment, or him, the slightest bit of attention. The ghost was entirely focused on the cat, the same fragile look on her face that made it clear she was overwhelmed by whatever portion of reality had just hit her. "I know that means I can keep it from hurting people, but if I could leave whenever I want to I would have done it already!" Lara told Sophia, voice wavering. "I've missed my family for so long!"

"I know you have, my dear." The cat's voice gentled. "But before now, you didn't *believe* you could leave. Until these gentlemen figured out how the ring worked, and proved you could control its power, your own certainty in your prison kept you trapped."

Lara's mouth fell open. "It can't be that simple."

"It can," Mandrake cut in. "Magic has the tendency to have really annoying loopholes like that."

Lara hesitated. "I could see my mother...." she whispered, almost too low to be heard. She blinked hard. "If she'd still been alive, I'm sure she never would have let me do something so foolish." She looked over at Waverly and Mandrake. "Do you think she'll forgive me?"

Waverly heard Mandrake murmur something comforting, his attention caught by Sophia. The cat had gone tense when Lara had talked about being able to see her mother, taking a step forward when she'd asked if her mother would forgive her. There was no reason for a cat to scheme to free a long-dead girl trapped in a ring, but Sophia had mentioned she'd already lived several lives....

"What do you say, Sophia?" Waverly asked, loudly enough to catch everyone's attention. "Will Lara's mother be able to forgive her?"

The cat's eyes immediately flicked to Waverly in a glare designed to burn him alive, but she flinched and looked back at Lara as the ghost moved closer. "Would she?" Lara asked. "Can you communicate with her, too?"

Mandrake, looking back and forth between Waverly and Sophia, got it more quickly than she did. "Let me guess. Did your mother used to refer to you as 'my dear?'"

Lara looked confused, Sophia annoyed, but they spoke at the same moment. "Yes, but that's hardly an uncommon...."

Their voices failed at nearly the same

time as Lara's eyes filled. "You always said that meant I really did have a magic power, because I could read your thoughts," she whispered, reaching out to the cat before she could stop herself.

"You are magic, my dear," Sophia whispered back, walking so that she passed just under Lara's ghostly fingers. "You always were."

Lara sniffled. "But if you're still alive, that means you won't be waiting for me."

Waverly stepped forward, clearing his throat to mask the suspicious tug of emotion in his chest. "If you have the power to believe yourself free, then you also have the power to choose to haunt your mother for the rest of her life," he said gently, drawing both their attention. "All you have to do is will it so."

Lara turned back to her mother. "Will it hurt you?"

Sophia shook her head. "Cats contain many lives." She brushed her nose in the space where the girl's palm was, as if nuzzling it. "And even if I didn't, I would always have room for you."

As she spoke the last word, light flared out from underneath the bandage partially covering the ring. When it died Waverly hurriedly started unwrapping the bandages, more surprised than he should have been to see gold-colored ash falling out. The last of it slipped away as the bandage did, leaving his injured finger bare and free.

Mandrake was the first one to break the silence. "Well, I suppose that was the universe saying it approves of the plan," he said brightly, turning back to Sophia and Lara. "Next time, would you *tell* us that you're about to suck us into a plan to free your ghost daughter?"

"Indeed." The severity he'd intended the word to have was ruined by the way his lips threatened to curve. "We prefer to go into these things prepared."

Sophia left her daughter only long enough to rub up against Waverly and Mandrake's legs in turn. "I have no more ghost daughters," she said, amused. "But you did what no one else has been able to before. I will do my best to spread word of your intelligence and resourcefulness."

"And kindness," Lara chimed in.

Mandrake winced. "Actually, can we keep that part a secret? We've got a reputation to uphold."

Waverly nodded. "Yes. Life is considerably easier if people believe the worst of us."

"Perhaps," Sophia said regally as she led her daughter away. "But the wise will always know better."

JENNIFFER WARDELL is a fantasy author whose novels include "Beast Charming," "Fighting Sleep," and "Fairy Godmothers, Inc. (Waverly and Manny's later adventures can be found in "Beast Charming.") She's also written several shorter works, including the humorous spy romances "How to Win Over Your Arch-Nemesis (In Three Easy Steps)" and "Dirty Deeds Done for Reasonable Prices."

Made in the USA
Las Vegas, NV
19 November 2020